Dodgefall

Can these two learn to play well
together on and off the field?

Ben Bisbee

Dedicated to my handsome, amazing, wildly tolerant husband, Joe, the love of my life.

And to Virginia Nelson, the first person to make me feel like a real author.

Dodgefall
by Ben Bisbee

Samuel loved living in DC for a variety of reasons as a Midwest transplant. There was always a networking event to attend, his job was fast and fulfilling, and it was always fun to treat the dating landscape like an overstuffed buffet.

Joining an adult kickball league was supposed to give him a reason to rub elbows with political staffers and nonprofit bigwigs, but he didn't anticipate it would lead to an unexpected date with Coach Easton.

And nothing could have prepared either of them after an awkward invitation to return to Samuel's hometown after just knowing each other a few weeks. Can these two learn to play well together on and off the field when the balls go flying?

Chapter One

Pulling a whitening strip from its thin, shimmering wrapper, Samuel considered his reflection in the bathroom mirror, sighing deeply, and tried to avoid a certain amount of self-shaming eye contact. He pressed the viscous, goo-covered veneer into the nooks and crannies of his perfect teeth with his forefinger and tongue, while leaning back carefully to peer out into his sundrenched bedroom.

What was his name again? James? John? Geoff? Regardless, the handsome brunette he'd met last night was dressing quickly in a hushed panic.

Little did the poor guy know—it was all part of the plan in the first place. Samuel liked to lie quietly awake until his guest awoke before quietly getting out of bed and into the bathroom, allowing this virtual stranger to hopefully—and almost always—quickly get assembled and discretely exit his apartment. Samuel didn't feel particularly good about any of it, but it wasn't without its own relief and rewards. Since moving to DC, it was fun to treat most of the city as a kind of boyfriend buffet.

Well, maybe not *boyfriend*. That was more than a few steps too far from the intended menu of things. Maybe back in Bloomington it made more sense to consider any date or one-night-stand as a potential boyfriend. Good looking gay guys were few and far between there. But in DC, he could attend any number of happy hours or special events taking place every single night and find half a dozen take-home options of the gay, bi, or gay-curious variety.

Samuel heard the front door close, allowing him to breathe out a bit and head into the kitchen to find something to rehydrate. Glancing out the kitchen window and down into the street below, he could see whatshisface still fixing his dark hair and buckling his braided belt while he headed away, likely toward the Metro station.

"He had a really nice ass." Samuel cooed to himself, before pouring some orange juice into his open mouth to avoid his constrained teeth.

"Did he now?" Rachel asked from behind him, startling Samuel and making him choke a little on the juice.

"Oh god, I didn't know you were up." Samuel croaked between coughs, feeling embarrassed because his roommate witnessed the entire series of events.

"You and I more alike than you realize, Sam. I also wait until these poor guys leave before showing my face or having some breakfast." Rachel poured some puffed rice cereal into a bowl and began eating it like popcorn—no milk, no spoon. "I know he rushed out of here, but why don't *you* have any pants on?"

Samuel grimaced a bit, shrugging while he chuckled, then attempted again to pour a bit more orange juice into his mouth, despite feeling exposed in his boxer briefs.

He'd be lying to himself if he pretended it was the first time his roommate caught him ushering some handsome bandit into the streets for their walk of shame. Shame didn't feel right to Samuel. He didn't feel any shame, nor he hoped would any of these guys. They both saw what they wanted, and they took the opportunity to indulge. Did he feel a little awkward sometimes—or foolish or frustrated or ambivalent—from time to time? Sure. But *shame* didn't need to be on the menu.

"What was wrong with this one?" Rachel asked, her mouth full of cereal.

He tried to find the words to explain. "Nothing? Nothing is wrong with any of them. This just is what it is. I'm young..."

Rachel rolled her eyes. "You're almost 31, Sam."

His brows popped up and he placed a hand on his chest for emphasis. "I'm perfectly *young* and have my whole world ahead of me. There is no need to rush into a big purchase in a city full of delightful rentals. Wait. That came out wrong. Not *rentals*. Whatever, you know what I mean. I don't owe someone who talks with their mouth full of food any explanations about class acts."

"Whatever you have to tell yourself, girl." Rachel laughed roughly, as she walked out of the kitchen and back into her bedroom, cereal bowl and spoon still in hand.

"I'm not telling myself anything, it's just the truth. And, for the millionth time, don't call me *girl*. I'm not that brand of gay." Samuel huffed in dramatic disgust, but his stomach roiled and the hollow sensation there wasn't just from skipping breakfast. He tried to tamp down on a sneaking suspicion his wounded feeling had more to do with her words than lack of food.

He'd date when he was ready, or so he'd been telling himself. After all, he'd only lived in DC for a handful of years, and there were still some neighborhoods he barely knew—why rush into a formal relationship just because of his age or how long he'd lived in the city?

Samuel finished swallowing the last of the orange juice and cracked his neck to the side, sighing again. Back in his room, he flipped open his laptop before pausing.

Do people just Google 'how to find a boyfriend?' or is that stupid? He knew it was stupid, and he didn't like how Rachel got into his head this early in the morning. She was his best friend, but she was also an annoying pain in the ass. His mother pushed the same topic literally every time they spoke, unfortunately. He didn't need *two* pushy women running the same lines over and over with him for a play he didn't want to perform.

Samuel closed his laptop and laid back on his bed, watching as the ceiling fan rotated slowly.

"I'm not unhappy." His jaw shifted.

His last real boyfriend was almost four years ago, back in Bloomington. In many ways, the end of that relationship provided the catalyst needed to push Samuel to pack up his entire life and move to DC. Michael was a great guy. A really great guy, honestly. They made a decent couple, but Samuel wasn't exactly a great boyfriend. Hyper, erratic, passionate-leaning-toward-overindulgent in his career in political fundraising, Samuel wanted to represent a kind of power couple image around their city. He wanted to be seen as the most important guy in the room and he felt it meant Michael riding along in a certain high-profile-side-saddle-dynamic to accomplish the narrative.

That wasn't Michael's pace or nature.

Michael was sweet, artsy, often aloof. He swung from being a quirky wallflower to spending all evening chatting boisterously with the event's catering chef or someone's elderly eccentric aunt who somehow made it onto the guest list. It was charming but challenging when it came to Samuel's vision of perceived success and prowess.

Their relationship lasted several years longer than it should have, but Samuel was determined, and Michael was in love. Maybe Samuel was, too? But he wasn't in love with how the relationship looked from the outside or how he felt it reflected on his influential image and networking efforts at the time.

Samuel thought about taking his talents to DC for a while before he broke it off with Michael. Every time he brought possibly moving up, Michael would laugh it off playfully, a bit of a townie move that irked Samuel. Michael often expressed how he couldn't imagine a life away from where he'd grown up, surrounded by all their friends and family.

One night, at a large fundraiser, Michael planned to meet up with Samuel a bit behind schedule, so he could still attend his pottery class. Samuel adored Michael's hobbies but never when they overlapped with his showcasing ambitions—Michael knew it, too. Arriving far later than expected, Michael had just playfully thrown on an ill-fitting suit jacket over his dirty, clay-stained overalls and short-sleeve button-down shirt.

Michael probably saw it as a testament to always being there for his boyfriend, even if the circumstances weren't ideal. For Samuel, it was the last straw.

That next morning, he broke it off. About six months later, Samuel found a part-time job in the heart of downtown DC, rented a small apartment in the suburbs, then left Indiana in the rearview mirror.

Within a few years, he became the head of fund development for a well-known east coast career Senator, overseeing a national staff of twenty-five, multiple large-scale events, and tens of millions of dollars in campaign and reelection funding.

He'd met Rachel early on at a hedge fund happy hour mixer where she was networking as a well-connected political investor liaison. With several things in common, they became fast friends, often accompanying each other at events as a pseudo power-couple, all the while never letting anyone forget Samuel was gay and Rachel was happily widowed. Well, Rachel wasn't *happy* her husband Phillipe died so young, leaving her a widow in her thirties—*fuck cancer*—but she seemed happy to avoid entertaining the idea of needing or wanting to date anyone new. Over time, they both determined they could afford a much nicer, modern apartment downtown if they pooled their money together as roommates. A few months later, they made it happen.

"Are you going to drag brunch today?" Rachel yelled across the apartment from her room.

Samuel glanced at his watch, realizing if he jumped in the shower, he could indeed make it in time. "I plan on going if you plan on going, but we'll be cutting it close."

"Then get your ass in gear and let's go."

Samuel slipped out of his underwear and into his large, marbled shower, focusing on his hot zones to be able to get ready fast enough to potentially jump in and out of several outfits before he found just the right one for brunch. After settling on a faded denim dress jacket, crisp white v-neck t-shirt and a pair of seersucker pants with navy loafers, Samuel felt ready to look summer smart and heavily available for brunch.

Rachel called for a driver, and they were out the door.

At the restaurant, the sidewalk was packed from edge to edge, making Samuel and Rachel grateful they always had tickets to these kinds of things, both of them knowing that every DC event—big or small—required you were either on the guest list or knew somebody in the room. Anything else meant being on the wait list—a sad situation they called the *free clinic*.

"Look at all those idiots waiting at the free clinic. Get tickets in advance, you tourists," Rachel scoffed as they walked past dozens of people waiting in line.

Tickets aside, the room was packed, making it complicated to find a table with two open seats. Thinking she found two, Rachel quickly sat down at nearby table, placing her purse in the other for Samuel, only to be told that the seat was already taken by someone at the bar ordering some drinks.

"I'm not getting up again." Rachel frowned a bit to feign guilt. Samuel rolled his eyes. Knowing the drill, he scanned the room for another open seat. Spotting one several tables over near the back of the room, he flipped Rachel off playfully before racing to try to grab the seat before someone else spotted it.

"This seat taken?" Samuel asked, quickly sitting down before anyone could say it wasn't available.

"Nope. It's all yours, bud," a sporty woman responded with a smile, slapping the tabletop loudly. "We've got company, folks."

The entire table of seven turned their attention to Samuel—all smiles and kind eyes saying hello.

"Hi..." Samuel said slowly and slightly amused by the synergy and energy of the crowd. "Do you all already know each other?"

"Yeah, we're all coaches with NUUDE Social Sports, here in town," one of the men answered. His eyes gleamed from being able to talk about his project with someone new. "I'm sure you've heard of us."

Samuel nodded, only needing a second to remember a bit about them. "Yeah, that's the co-ed amateur sports league, right? Cornhole, flag football, kickball, that kind of thing?" Samuel often spotted various teams of people in matching t-shirts playing all sorts of ridiculous children's games all over the city, especially around the National Mall grounds.

"Exactly, my friend." The man nodded, taking a bite of a random pastry from a mixed basket on the table. "We're all part of the LGBTQ+ leagues, specifically. Have you ever thought about joining a league?"

Samuel smirked. If anyone knew the power of the casual salesmanship of DC mimosa networking, it was him, but he didn't come to drag brunch to be pitched the value of adult play sociability. Well, or at least not of the *sports* variety.

While he valued fitness and athleticism, he couldn't imagine dragging himself to a grassy corner outside a Smithsonian to high-five strangers over a game of giant Jenga. *Saturday mornings are for waving off Friday night dates, catching up on trashy reality television, and planning the week ahead with more pressing events and networking options in esteemed, high-rise settings.*

Aloud, he only said, "Ha. No. Nope. I mean, I hear they're fun and rewarding, and I like a good competition, but that's really not my kind of scene." Samuel did his best to look earnest and apologetic to avoid insulting any of his tablemates while still making it clear he wasn't biting.

"Yeah, that's what all the DC young professionals say until they kick their first ball into the stupid face of a deserving Congressional aide. You know what I mean?" The table laughed in agreement.

"Last week, I watched the Communications Director of the National Red Cross full-on tackle a regulatory lobbyist to the ground before *conveniently* remembering they were playing flag football," a woman with red braids shared gleefully.

The guy next to him gave Samuel an elbow nudge before adding, "Earlier in the season, I saw the VP of Philanthropy at the Democracy Fund thumb wrestle one of the Arizona Senator's press secretary—and lose. Next thing you know, I'm reading about Senator Jabrowski getting the second largest gift I've ever seen from the DF. We're more than just sports, you know?"

"Huh. You don't say." Samuel relaxed, sipping on his table mimosa, "So, it's just slick networking hiding out as silly sports?"

"No, my friend." A thin, handsome Black man across the table winked at Samuel, then explained, "It's a social sporting experience firstly. One that often turns into far more, especially in this city. But we take the sports—even the sillier ones—as seriously as whatever happens after the games."

Samuel nodded quickly. "No, I get it. I do. I never thought of it like that. I always assumed it was intended as a break from the grind, not just another version of it."

"NUUDE Sports is like DC itself. How you want to connect with the city matters, but at the end of the day, everything is still political in nature, and sometimes that comes down to who you know. You know?" The man retorted.

"No trust me, *I know*." Samuel laughed, fully picking up what this group was putting down. He leaned in, conspiratorially asking, "So, do you all always leave one seat open at events like this to trick unsuspecting bystanders like me into the game?"

Everyone at the table laughed.

"Sports are sports, man," a hot Asian guy said with a laugh. "And if you love them, you play them anywhere you happen to be, bystanders beware."

Chapter Two

After brunch, the room emptied, spilling Rachel and Samuel into the street to find their driver for the ride home.

Rachel shook her head as she waved to their driver across the street. "Ha. You are absolutely not joining one of those stupid sports groups."

"I don't know. Who knows? I just might." Samuel shrugged, feeling still relatively fifty-fifty about the entire venture, which was fifty percent more than he'd ever dreamed he would likely feel about the subject. "You should have heard their stories, Rach. Congressional staff, fundraisers, high ranking foundation executives—all of them playing kickball as far as the public was concerned, while working a dozen little high-level side deals under the table. Sounds pretty dreamy. Minus the kickball, I mean."

Rachel shook his arm as if she could physically joggle the idea out of him. "Do you even hear yourself? Joining a kickball ball league while hating kickball to network during kickball." She climbed into the car with a huff that sounded weary of the discussion.

Samuel also got in the car then thanked the driver for picking them up and confirmed their address. Once that was taken care of, he turned back to Rachel, holding his hands up in defense before she could even start. "No, I *know*. I hear myself just fine. I always thought they were really into sports, not people who might love to network secretly while using sports as a decoy. I don't know how I didn't realize sooner, frankly."

Rachel collapsed back into her seat, covering her eyes with her hand. "Because it's kickball, Sam. *Kickball*."

He sniffed out an annoyed puff of air. "Oh god, *stop*. They have other sports."

"Right. Like *dodgeball*," Rachel agreed, narrowing her eyes at him.

Samuel didn't answer, but unease joined the embarrassment heating his cheeks. Part of him agreed with her—it *was* stupid. His stomach churned, his mimosa hating how right she probably was. That part of himself would *love* to die of humiliation on the spot for even bringing up the idea of joining NUUDE.

The other part of himself—the part that didn't agree with her—remembered how people in his small town thought he'd never make it in the city. They all thought it was a crazy idea, but his gut said to try anyway... As he watched the familiar buildings fly by out the window, all towering grey and steel, he still thought he might give the sport group a chance, too.

Rachel could read his expressions pretty well after being friends for so long, so he wasn't surprised when she said, "No. Sam, just no. It's not worth it. You know I'm right."

With a sigh, he admitted, "I'm just going to *one* dodgeball game. Just one. Just to see. That's all."

"Dodgeball? Really? That's the one you picked?" Her tone dripped sarcasm.

"Oh shut up. I used to really like that game in grade school. And I sucked at it, but I'm older now, far more fit, wildly more put together. I'd like to think it's my turn to hurl a ball at someone's head and not be called a faggot in return." He joked, but it would be nice.

Rachel's brow popped up, her lips curling in amusement. "Well, when you put it like that..."

Excited because at least she was listening, he added, "Plus, they have all-gay leagues, so I'm joining one of those. This team's t-shirts are apparently sage green—a color I look good in, no matter the hue. If, along the way, I can rub elbows with a high-end donor or foundation lead? It's all pretty win-win to at least put my toe in the water."

She reached out and caught his hand, giving it a squeeze before saying, "Yeah, well, just try not to drown, okay? A group of gay men throwing balls at each other in public? It sounds like Pride Jazz Fest in the park last year after someone slipped MDNA in the punch."

He stuck his tongue out at her. "You suck. You're not wrong, but you suck." Unable to hold it in any longer, Samuel laughed.

She joined him, but after a moment caught his arm to add, "Oh. And before you even think to ask? No. Absolutely not."

"No what?" he asked, hoping his expression remained innocent.

Rachel shook her head. "I won't be one of your cheerleaders or offer to bring orange slices for the team. Never. Don't ask, don't beg, don't even expect me to attend a single game. What you do to ruin your Saturday mornings is on *your* time, not mine."

He ran his tongue across his teeth before answering. "Fine. But you're still going to have to stitch me up if I get any injuries. Nurse me back to health."

She gave it all of ten solid seconds of deep consideration. "Never. Maybe I'd consider signing your cast, but even that feels out of character this early in the fantasy."

"God, I hate you," Samuel said with a genuine smile.

She batted her lashes, dramatizing her sadness. "Which leaves me a little emotionally bruised after hearing how much you hate other things yet can't seem to stop yourself from still doing them," Rachel teased as they arrived at their building.

Later in the afternoon, Samuel sat on the edge of his bed, staring blankly at his laptop screen. He let his hands float a bit anxiously over the keys, still wondering if really did want to sign up for NUUDE Sports. On one hand, it could offer a fascinating new gateway for political and philanthropic schmoozing. On the other, it was public dodgeball for the world to see on the edge of the Capitol Building.

Samuel took a deep breath and clicked on the *Register Now* button to create a profile and pay for his spot on the team. After filling everything out, he hit send and closed his laptop. *Did I just fall for a recruitment scam?*

At worst, he'd attend one game, play a few rounds, hate it, meet no one of value, and still have a solid story to pick apart for other's amusement at the next proper mixer. In most ways, it was all pretty win-win, even if he lost.

Samuel's phone rang. A glance at his screen told him it was his mother. He stared at the phone, debating if he would answer or let her go to voicemail. Calls from his mother cut both ways—she guilt tripped him about moving out of the Midwest, while he guilted her for not being more supportive of his accomplishments in the big city. Neither of them ever left the call feeling as if they accomplished much.

Samuel answered on the third ring to send a silent passive-aggressive message. "Hey mom."

"Oh, I wasn't sure if you would be available," she responded tightly, lobbing the passive-aggression back like a tree dropping a branch on one of its' own fallen apples.

He flopped back on his bed and reached for a pillow. "Nope, just relaxing after having brunch with Rachel."

"You're exhausted from having brunch?" He heard the censure in the spaces between her words—rest and self-care, after all, were the bane of the average Midwesterner.

Samuel paused to unclench his jaw a bit, unsure if he should respond directly or just change the subject. After all, he knew that she wasn't asking a question of merit. "How are you?" he asked instead.

"Fine. And your father says hello. You know him on a Saturday afternoon, Sammy. He's out working in the garage or the basement or the yard. I'm entirely unsure on what or where, but he's happy, so I'm happy. He sends his love." Her clipped tone made him wonder why she'd bothered to call at all.

"Sure." Samuel didn't argue, but he always assumed his mother knew exactly what his father was doing and where, despite her proclaimed confusion. Then again, since he and his father hadn't really talked in over a decade, who cared?

"But I'm fine. I've been trying to get in more walks these days, you know, as Dr. Patel keeps recommending. He's been saying it ever since the holidays. For my health. So, I do, I go. Sometimes to the mall, sometimes at the Natatorium, if it's not too busy or overrun with teenagers lunging about everywhere. When I feel up to it, I even visit the marketplace and do a bit of shopping along the way." Her tone got increasingly sing-songy, making Samuel feel something anxiety-inducing was forthcoming.

With his fist clenched to stem his rising nerves, he said, "Well, that all sounds good, mom. Dr. Patel certainly wouldn't be asking you to walk if it wasn't for you."

"Oh, sure, sure, of course. I trust that man implicitly. Anyway, the market has really changed since you were here last. I can't even recall what they had when you were last here. Did you know they have a full florist now? And a Tahitian rolled ice cream place?"

"Thai."

"What?" Samuel's mother accused more than asked.

Samuel explained, "It's *Thai* rolled ice cream, not Tahitian. Tahiti is part of French Polynesia; Thailand is entirely different, altogether."

"Right. But they're essentially neighbors, I'm sure, right?"

Samuel chuckled quietly. "No, thousands of miles away from one another actually. Different oceans, even."

"Fine, sure. No matter. It's rolled ice cream. Delightful nonetheless."

"I get it, mom." Samuel sighed, feeling heavy on the feather comforter.

"Well, no matter. *The point of all of this* is that I bumped into Michael. At the marketplace. At the new florist shop."

The line went silent. His mother probably stayed silent to revel in her dramatic conversation killer while he tried to recover from the cold slice of her words.

"Yeah?" Samuel finally squeaked. He didn't regret breaking up with Michael three years ago, but he knew when his mother "bumped into" or mentioned Michael, the shame train was chugging downhill.

His mother continued, as if she thought he'd want to hear more. "Oh sure, of course I see him from time to time around town or at the grocery store. Such a sweet young man. I believe he was buying flowers for his new beau. I don't recall his name, of course, and I didn't want to pry."

Samuel sighed. "Last I heard he was dating a nice guy named Oliver."

"We chatted about you a bit. He asked, of course. I wouldn't assume he'd want to know otherwise, but I filled him in."

"On *what*? About what?" Samuel's face felt hot. He wished he sent her to voicemail after all.

Her condescending tone grated on his nerves as she said, "That you're doing your best in DC working for a Senator you like. That you're with a roommate but aren't dating anyone that I know of. Just the stuff I know firsthand. Nothing more, nothing less. Don't get upset."

"I'm not upset, Mom..." Samuel trailed off.

Although she frequently framed things from a place of inaccurate vulnerability, she wasn't technically wrong about anything she told Michael. If he suggested she should reframe things or got her tone or adjectives wrong, she'd just press him about other, unwanted topics. Basically, nothing he could say would be the right thing, so better to stick to the vague responses.

He said, "Sounds like you filled him in pretty well. And good for him and Oliver. They sound great together. I'm happy for them. and I'd hope he's feels the same for me."

"He didn't say one way or the other. He mostly thanked me for remembering him and said how he always enjoyed—*and missed*—talking to me. Which was sweet, don't you think?"

Another fake question. He wasn't falling for it.

"I'm always happy when you're happy, Mom." Samuel laid back on his bed, holding the phone against one hear while massaging his face with his other hand.

"Alright, well that was about it. Nothing more interesting to report on from here in the bleak Midwest."

"Appreciate the call as always, mom."

"Uh-huh, well don't forget the phone works in both directions, Sammy."

"I won't. Love you."

"Love you too and so does Dad."

"Yep, you said. Love you, Mom. Bye."

"Bye, Sammy." With that, the line went appropriately dead.

Samuel scooched to the edge of the bed before shaking his head as if he could free himself from his own thoughts with the motion. He didn't regret breaking up with Michael the person, but he did regret not being in a close relationship. He missed the easy intimacy, the comfort of being part of us rather than a party of one.

No matter how much he might miss the intimacy, he didn't date in a more traditional fashion anymore—not because he was heartbroken about Michael, but because it didn't fit his goals and lifestyle.

For the most part.

Dating was hard. Trying to navigate a top-tier profession in his industry was hard. One-night stands and casual relationships were easy, plain and simple. Well, simple aside from his guilt and anxiety and the tangential loneliness he tried to ignore.

One thing was certain—he was done taking calls from his mother for a few weeks.

Chapter Three

Dressing for the sporting event was almost as stressful as considering attending in the first place. Should he wear his active wear down to edge of the National Mall?

No. He couldn't bear the thought of getting picked up by a driver in casual sports shorts and a t-shirt. *Never.* There wasn't any place around the Capital building to change, so what if he wore jeans over his shorts? Should he bring a bag? How much would he sweat, actually? Should he bring a full change of clothing? Would they be going to bar afterward? That seemed likely, but he didn't want to show up at a bar sweaty and gross wearing a grubby t-shirt and shorts.

In the car, Samuel felt uneasy about his choice to wear a pair of lightweight travel pants over his basketball shorts, a zipped-up hoodie over his t-shirt, his running shoes and a brand new name brand bag. He'd filled the bag with four different outfits to choose from depending on where they went after the game, complete with a crisp white shirt and tie...just in case.

Samuel hoped there would be water or something to drink at the event itself, because he didn't have room for any drinks and didn't want any of his other clothing to get wet from condensation. *What if I have to pee? Are there bathrooms nearby for changing, even?*

Maybe this was a mistake.

Maybe he should ask the driver to pull over so he could get out. He could safely walk a few blocks away then call another car, hoping this one didn't think it was personal or worse, drove over to pick him back up by mistake, forcing him to explain this ridiculous ordeal. Before he could even make a formal decision about escaping, the car arrived at the southwest side of the Mall lawn, his destination.

Dozens of individuals wandered around in various colored NUUDE shirts, including a few in the sage green he was promised to receive at the game. Samuel thanked the driver reluctantly and hopped out, feeling instantly uneasy and foolish—*like the first day at a new school, showing up in the middle of the year.*

Seeing a concentration of sage green shirts a few hundred yards away, he made the slow, awkward trek into the side lawn to meet his fate and cross the experience off his list. He resisted the urge to run or jog over like a nerd, so the long walk across the field felt like torture.

He introduced himself to hyper group of younger men stretching their legs on the grass and joking with one another. "Hi. Um, I think I'm here for the dodgeball game? I'm Samuel."

One offered a hand to shake and said, "Hey, welcome, Samuel. Very cool, man. I'm Rich, and this is Jason and Brian. We're with Hertzog, Warner, and Roberts. Where are you from, where do you work?"

The two classic, iconic, essential DC questions: *Where are you from?* and *Where do you work?* The first one wasn't related to where a person lived in the city, but where they "originally" came from or moved from, since a massive contemporary population of DC's working class—white and blue collar alike—weren't typically from DC proper. The second question explained how they ended up in the city in the first place, because most people moved to DC for a job.

Familiar with the routine, Samuel said, "I'm from Indiana, and I'm the National Fundraising Director for Senator Marcus."

"Very cool. Awesome, bud. We just finished a case with Senator Rickowski, actually." Rich smiled, putting out his fist for a bump.

It felt very bro-dude and unqueer, but Samuel expected as much from DC. The lines of what gay people "looked like" or "acted like" got very blurry. Stereotypes weren't consistent or pervasive in the District, but he still wanted to make sure he wasn't in the wrong place.

"This is the LGBTQ League, right?" Samuel asked bluntly.

"Yep. We're team SAGE: Sexuality And Gender Equality. You're in the right place, bud." Rich winked knowingly. "You'll want to get checked in with our Team Leader, Easton. He's a self-described Blasian—big built, handsome guy over by the equipment if you were looking for a bit more specificity." Rich pointed toward a much larger group of men and women in matching shirts about ten yards away.

"Blaisan?" Samuel chuckled; pretty sure he understood the term but wanting to confirm.

"Black Asian." Jason or Brian responded smiling.

"Gotcha. Cool, thanks guys." Samuel waved slightly, heading in the direction of the group, feeling a bit more confident.

The group of clustered sage green shirts were a mix of about twelve men and women of a pretty diverse set of ages and races talking in a circle about the game. Samuel stayed a few feet away to scan the group for Easton.

Like some kind of cartoon prince, the guy had a deeply chiseled jaw and gorgeous brown eyes—just that perfect combo of sexy and pretty. Samuel bit his lip as his gaze slid past Easton's enormous muscular shoulders and a carved physique. This man didn't miss leg day. The circle of people began breaking apart, snapping Samuel out of his consideration of Prince Hottie. Samuel stepped forward to quickly introduce himself.

"Easton?" Samuel asked. His hands went a bit clammy, and his throat tightened.

"That's me." Easton smiled brightly, filling the air with even more sunshine.

He waved goodbye to one of the teammates before striding to offer Samuel a proper handshake. He hoped his hand wasn't moist, but he was impressed by the firm grip in response. Then Easton put his other hand on Samuel's shoulder for an extra gesture of warm welcome.

"Um. Hey. Hi. I'm Samuel. Sam," Samuel stammered. He felt flushed and wildly out of his element for some reason.

"It's nice to meet you, Sam. Are you joining SAGE today, I hope? Did anyone get you a t-shirt yet?" Easton held Samuel's shoulder lightly even as their hands dropped, pushing the butterflies in Samuel's belly to do a few fancy flips and spins.

Easton called over to another player asking them to bring over a men's medium shirt. "That'll work right? You're pretty fit. Did you find us online or were you tricked into showing up from one of our bar appearances?"

"Me? Oh, I was attacked at brunch last weekend." Samuel laughed, feeling himself blush.

A team member handed a shirt to Easton, who then passed it to Samuel. Samuel hoped their hands might slightly touch in the transaction, but they didn't.

"Ah, yes, that's another of our prime hunting grounds. Good, good, it's all working, all this hunting and gathering from the natural springs." Easton winked, making Samuel's knees buckle a bit.

Samuel blurted, "Well, you trapped me. I'm all yours." Immediately he realized how it would sound, then his eyes went wide.

Easton seemed to take it in stride, and he gave Samuel's shoulder a brief squeeze. "Ha. Well, no worries just yet. We're not unkind to our prey at first. Let's get you in that t-shirt. We're about to do a full team huddle. We'll do introductions, explain the rules, then we'll talk about team placement. You know, the boring stuff."

"I don't mind the boring stuff." Samuel said, hoping he sounded interested.

"Then you're a better man than me, Sam, my friend." Easton squeezed Samuel's shoulder one last time before rejoining the group. He blew his commanding whistle to gather everyone into their team circle. Samuel watched him walk away, tracking his thick thighs pushing against his white athletic shorts, his apple-smooth calves, and impressive bubble butt.

For the first time, Samuel understood the culture governing the need to pat a fellow player's butt in-between scores and... *innings? Quarters? What on earth does dodgeball even have?* Samuel supposed he'd learn soon enough or fake it along the way.

When he joined the team huddle, it became clear that although dodgeball in elementary school just meant trying to avoid getting hit too quickly, their strategy focused on actual plays, designed defensive measures, and constantly accessing the other team's weaknesses for opportunities. It might be famed as fun, playful, joyful, but it was also absolutely being taken seriously as a sport under the clear umbrella of *winning*.

Samuel considered himself fit, but he certainly wasn't athletic. Ten minutes out on the field left him panting and sweating. Despite the sweat, he bobbed and weaved, threw balls, caught and tried his best to dodge projectiles during the game.

Numbers on the backs of shirts distinguished the teams—as well as making it easy to remember which sage shirt to re-connect with off the field. Samuel wore the number thirty but found himself particularly attentive if Easton shouted out a play or maneuvers. So, when Easton was instead calling out his *name* every play, instead of his number, it was a little reward.

"Sam, go left, buddy! Good job, great work, Sam. Way to snipe that ball." Easton yelled, making Samuel's skin tingle.

He loved being called into action, knowing Easton focused on his every move in those moments. Each time Easton used his first name, the little frisson of awareness sizzled down Samuel's spine, pooling in his loins like a pulse of sexual awareness. In fact, there were a few moments when the combination of hearing his name being shouted by Easton mixed with a careful eye on Easton's amazing butt and thighs required Samuel to actually focus on the game in order to avoid an unwanted public erection.

All too soon, the game ended. His team only won by one point, but a win was a win, and everyone was in great spirts. Plans to head to a local bar to pull back some drinks and celebrate a little over some deeper, less casual networking began erupting around Samuel.

"Sam, you joining us at the bar?" Easton asked, as he packed things up around the field. Samuel felt the back of his neck sweat a bit off-field.

"I am if you are?" Samuel shrugged, trying to seem a bit coy, a bit flirty.

"I can't make it. Well, not this week, but I encourage you to go. A big part of NUUDE is the after-parties and networking. The game is just a high-energy primer, you know?" Easton zipped up a bag and then began counting equipment. His tan, bulging arms tightened into balls of ripped muscles each time he closed a new bag. Samuel was a bit stunned, unprepared to have to wait another week or more to get some face time with the fascinating man.

"Are you sure you can't come out for a bit? One drink? On me? For helping to coach me into a winner on my first game?" Samuel sounded a bit more desperate than he liked, losing a bit of his cooler, flirty charm.

"Nah. No, not today, Sam. Sorry. I've got to get this stuff dropped off on the other side of the city." Easton shrugged, pulling several heaving sports bags over his bulging shoulders.

"What part of the city? I don't care where I buy you that beer. Maybe I can help you out with all the equipment then we'll find a place closer to where you're headed? Just the two of us?" Samuel bit his lip at this last statement, realizing he was stupidly showing all his cards.

Easton paused for a moment, looking down for a moment before raising his head with a sly smile.

"Ok, sure. Yeah. Sure. I'd like that." He smiled, lowering his eyes a bit to the floor, as the city spun gently around him.

Chapter Four

Samuel offered to grab them both a ride, both for the intimacy and with the several bags of equipment in mind, but Easton was intent on them taking the Metro instead.

"With all these bags?" Samuel scoffed.

"Ah, you're one of those guys, huh?" Easton smiled coyly, handing a few bags to Samuel before heading toward the nearby Metro Station Yellow/Green Line.

"What? No. I mean, not really? It's just easier sometimes, or with several bags of sporting equipment, you know?" Samuel tried laughing it off, unsure why Easton wouldn't just take his kind offer of convenience and comfort.

"No, I know. I just like the Metro. Always have. Besides, it is only a few stops then just off the Station. You'll be fine, Sam." Easton tossed a wink over his shoulder like a breadcrumb for the hungry Samuel to enjoy.

"So, you've been in the city for a while?" Samuel asked, trying to change the subject.

"All my life." Easton replied, still moving swiftly.

"Oh, wow, that's so rare." Samuel said. It was—most of the people Samuel met were imports like him who came to the city for work as adults.

Easton shot Samuel a playful glare, cocking his head. "We're not an endangered species, my friend."

Samuel's eyes widened as he immediately worried he'd offended the other man. "No, sorry, right. I just mean, you really don't meet a lot of folk from DC in DC, you know?

"Sure you do, you just have to stop hanging out with mostly transient people who aren't from DC to know better, you know?" Easton laughed, the sound breaking the tension, before returning to his easy, long stride, "Speed it up, Sam, or we're going to miss the coming train. Don't get too far behind."

Samuel quickly regretted his decision. With every action, every sentence, he felt more like an outsider, awkward and unsure of how what he said, or thought, might land. But damn, Easton was hot, and frankly very kind. *Not the worst option to spend my afternoon chasing a date, but it certainly isn't going how I hoped.*

Once they entered L'Enfant Plaza Metro Station, Easton waved Samuel to match his slight jog so they could both catch the front car moments from closing its doors. Once inside, they both collapsed into a four-seater with their multiple bags of equipment spread between them. The car was quiet, with only a few folks sprinkled within the metallic space.

"Whew, we almost missed it." Easton reached over the bags to pat Samuel on his thigh. An electric rollercoaster traveled up Samuel's leg, dancing a bit across his groin and stomach, before ending at his heart. That last stop wasn't quite as expected as the others.

"Where are we headed?" Samuel asked, feeling a bit dizzy.

"Congress Heights. Green line." Easton offered no other information.

"Southeast, ok." Samuel replied, hoping for more.

Easton laughed. "It's not as rough as I'm sure you've heard or been warned about."

"What I don't know about southeast DC would likely shock you, Easton." Samuel replied with a chuckle, hoping it would open up a little conversation.

"Oh, a virgin, very cool." Easton winked, smirking.

"In a very loose manner of speaking," Samuel responded, but he felt the heat flood his cheeks.

Within a few minutes, they arrived at the Congress Heights metro. Once they got off the train, they headed up the escalator to the street level. Anxiety grew like a bubble inside Samuel, and he sensed it from Easton, but he couldn't pinpoint why. Despite the rising tension, he was at least along for the ride and alone with Easton—a win in his book.

"So where are we heading to?" he asked when the tension forced the question past his breathless lips.

Easton didn't seem winded in the least by the labor after heavy exercise. "We're going to stop by my Auntie's to drop off this equipment and check in with her. Afterward, we can head to a nearby bar I like in the neighborhood. Sound ok?"

"Yeah, absolutely, as long as it's ok with you." He felt like a third wheel in this adventure of two.

"I wouldn't have dragged you along if it wasn't, Sam." Easton smiled, pulling him over by the shoulder a bit into his own tight shoulder, playfully.

Another butterfly fluttered its way around Samuel's stomach and heart, much to his dismay. *What the hell is wrong with me?* His mood seemed odd and unlike himself. Easton was hot, he was hot, they were both single guys—as far as he knew—and they were just going on a little afternoon date. Nothing new. So why did this feel so weird and gross? Was he maybe coming down with something? A twenty-four-hour flu or a touch of sour stomach? Did one game of dodgeball kick his ass that hard?

A few blocks from the Metro, Easton stopped short in front of a classic grey, two story brick rowhouse outside of the unshackled gate. He sighed before turning to Samuel.

"This is it, my Auntie's place. Just a fair warning—She's... Well." Easton trailed off, seeming to struggle to find his words, "She might pay you no mind, she might ask a million little questions. I wouldn't read much into either scenario." Although he smiled, the expression read as uneasy.

"I get it." Samuel knew his mother could behave very similar.

"Yeah, and, um, if she mentions–? ...You know what? Never mind. Let's just see what's kind of day she's having then I can sort things out as needed." Easton laughed awkwardly, a sound that did nothing to alleviate Samuel's rising anxiety.

Easton unlocked and opened the front door, yelling for his Auntie who didn't answer. Waving Samuel inside, they both walked into a living room filled with outdated layers of brown furniture and more than one tube television. Easton yelled for his aunt again, before a large gorgeous black woman in a flowered house dress and curlers rounded the corner from the kitchen.

"What, Easton?" She bellowed, looking slightly aggravated.

"Just didn't want to scare you, Auntie. We're here to drop off the kickball equipment and then down to Lowery's for a drink." He smiled at her, genuine love shining in his gorgeous dark eyes.

"We? Who's *we*?" Her gimlet gaze landed on Samuel with an added arched eyebrow.

"This is Sam." Easton replied, "Sam, meet is my Auntie Regina. He just joined the SAGE league, so we're going to get a drink to celebrate our win today."

"Just you two, huh?" Her gaze remained steadily on Samuel. He focused rather desperately not to squirm under the weight of her regard.

"Yep, just us." Samuel said but his tone sounded a bit confused.

"So, he's gonna be cool? He knows and everything?" Auntie Regina pried.

Easton sighed. "Auntie, stop. It's not like that. It's just a drink to celebrate." Easton hushed her before heading up the stairs. He waved the still pinned Samuel to join him with the bags. Auntie Regina didn't release him from her stare, so Samuel stayed in place, uncertain.

"Sam?" Easton called again from the top of the stairs.

The new tension in his tone snapped Samuel out of it. "Um. Right. I'm coming."

Auntie Regina nodded then watched him climbing the stairs before retreating back into the kitchen. At the top of the stairs, Samuel froze again, unsure which way to go to find Easton down the long hallway of identical opened doorways.

"Second room on the right," Easton called, "Just drop the bags then we can get going."

The room was also outdated, like a child's room from a least a decade ago—monkey sheets on a twin bed, posters of boy bands and movie stars, daisy curtains, lots of yellow and pink pillows alongside a phone charger, alarm clock, and shelves filled with girl's sporting awards and trophies.

"Your bedroom, I assume?" Samuel joked, trying to cut some tension.

"Oh. Um. Ah. Not anymore?" Easton replied, acting a bit like water poured on a robot, before swiftly walking past Samuel and back into the open hallway. "You coming?"

"Yeah. Of course." Samuel replied, unsure what just happened.

Flying down the stairs, Easton shot straight to the door, waving Samuel over to hurry.

"Bye, Auntie!" He yelled but didn't wait for a response before closing the door behind them. He hurried out of the front yard and once again on to the empty sidewalk.

Chapter Five

Most of the trip to the bar, silence reigned. Each fast step ramped the uncomfortable tension higher, but Samuel still wasn't sure of the cause. At a crosswalk, Easton finally broke the tension with the words, "Sorry, that was weird."

"Nothing to apologize for, man. It wasn't that weird," Samuel lied.

"It was. She is. But I love my Auntie. She basically raised me since I was a tween." Easton admitted, before pushing forward again to cross the street.

"Do you want to talk about it? Because you don't have to. You can if you want to," Samuel said softly, not want to push a topic that already felt guarded, but not wanting to be misunderstood.

"Probably not tonight, if you don't mind." Easton stopped for a moment, looking down at his feet. "I know we've only just met, and this isn't a date-date, but, well, I feel like the deeper, darker stuff, the family stuff, the past-is-in-the-past stuff? Can wait a few more dates, maybe."

"Deeper, darker, huh?" Samuel laughed. "A few *more* dates, huh?"

"I'm totally screwing this up, aren't I?" Easton rubbed his handsome face in embarrassment.

But he wasn't. *Not even in the least bit.* Samuel was so dialed in, he had no idea how or why, but he was oddly relieved that Easton even jokingly mentioned more dates at all.

"Nope. Not yet anyway, handsome." Samuel smiled, placing a trembling hand on Easton's tight shoulder. He hoped to drive the message and his reassurance home.

Easton's brow rose. "Oh good, I still have some wiggle room to mess it up."

Samuel's lips twitched, but he managed to keep a serious tone when he replied, "Well, at least enough for me to buy you that beer I promised. We still have some celebrating to do."

They arrived at Lowery's—a bit a dive, but the kind of outdated, classic bar DC was oddly famous for. Stoic, tall multi-colored brick interior walls rose above rich mahogany wood and leather everywhere. Towering, stately, stiff booths were littered with pretty fantastic looking drinks paired with fairly uninspired snacks. Easton grabbed a booth in the back and they both sat down.

"So now you know where I'm from, tell me about where you're from?"

Samuel scanned the menu before answering easily. "Bloomington, Indiana, born and raised, just a bit south of Indianapolis. But I've been in the District for just over three years."

They ordered drinks and perused the available snacks before Easton picked the conversation back up where they'd left off.

"And you like it?" Easton snagged a pretzel, taking it between his lush lips before snapping a bit off and chewing thoughtfully.

Samuel licked his lips before answering. "I love it. Its everything I wanted—busy, bustling, filled with interesting people, exhibits and museums plus networking, politics and advancement opportunities. I head up the fund development team for Senator Marcus from Ohio."

"Fancy." Easton cooed over his beer.

For long moments, they simply gazed into one another's eyes. Heat rose in Samuel's cheeks, but he noticed a similar tell-tale blush staining Easton's cheeks. Their drinks arrived, breaking the moment, but Samuel darted another quick glance at Easton to find the man still looking back from beneath long, dark lashes.

Samuel took a reassuring sip of his beer before he managed to find words again. "Fancy enough, I suppose. And you? Just a full-time volunteer coach for NUUDE sports or something more exciting paying your bills?"

Easton reached for another pretzel. "I'm in development, but on the program side. At Theresa's Table."

Samuel's smile came easy and naturally rather than being forced. "Oh, I *love* them. They do so much cool work for the homeless and

LGBTQIA+ community at large. Very cool. What kind of stuff are you running over there?"

Easton waved his pretzel like a baton as he answered, "I'm the managing director of outreach services, with a focus on our educational programs, engagement, mission and psychological programs, the pantry...those sorts of things. All the stuff that helps stabilize folks or supports their needs for pushing folks forward. Blah blah."

Samuel reached across the table to touch Easton's arm. Although the smooth, muscled skin under his hand struck him as warm and firm enough for further investigations, he instead focused on his words after giving the other man a reassuring squeeze. "No, not *blah blah*, man. that organization is beloved. I've only been here a few years yet I've never heard anything but great things. I've even donated at the grocery register and dropped off some unused clothing I didn't need last year for your clothing pantry."

Easton smiled coyly. "I thought my favorite dress shirt I snagged last year smelled familiar."

"Ah, well, good to know it went to such a good cause, and on such a great body, might I add." Samuel offered, feeling a bit looser as he finished off his first glass of cider.

"Well, thank you. I try to take care of myself. So, tell me, what's been your very favorite thing about DC so far, Sam?"

Samuel's brain paused for a second, fighting the urge to say "you" in both earnest and for fear of sounding too drunk or too flippant or flirtatious.

What is wrong with me? Of course, Easton was handsome, kind, smart, thoughtful, and compassionate. but he wasn't the first guy with most of those assets Samuel met or even dated. In fact, Samuel threw several prize-worthy fish back into the sea recently. Willingly, happily.

No, his reactions to Easton were different, but an indescribable different. He felt hot, cold, anxious, confident, eager, fearful, horny, timid—all at the same time. He wanted their date to never end, but he also wanted to run screaming far, far away. The combination left him feeling stupid and bold, vulnerable and empowered. *Like having the worse food poisoning while being ravenously hungry for more.*

Instead of admitting any of it, Samuel went with a safer answer. "I want to say the National Portrait Museum, because every time I go, I feel like I see something, feel something different, you know?"

Easton nodded. "Such a good museum, I know. Fully agree."

Samuel blew out a breath, and words finally flowed. "But, if I'm being honest? This woman is always at the same corner of the same block where I wait the light before crossing the street to get to my office. Her name is Nevaeh. She's not too much older than us. She's homeless, but she also works for the local homeless newspaper. Several times a week, I stop, and we chat. She knows my name; I know hers. I know her mom has custody of her kids, and she sees them once a month. She loves the rain and hates the direct sunshine. She's funny, and witty, and she always asks me about how work is going. I always have a twenty to hand her and she's stopped thanking me for it. I don't mind because I know she's always grateful since we're kind of friends, if that doesn't sound crazy."

The genuine smile—the one that melted something in Samuel's spine—graced Easton's perfect face. "Not at all, it's actually very sweet."

Samuel smiled, imagining Nevaeh's face. "Yeah. Nevaeh is kind of my favorite thing. Person. But now that I said that, it feels wrong, like I'm patronizing her or dehumanizing her. I don't mean it like that. I mean, our weird friendship, our weekly interactions, they're my favorite thing, I guess. She's just lovely."

Samuel called over to the bartender for another round and plate of their cheese sticks.

"No, I like that. I get that. She sounds great. I completely understand what you mean, on all accounts. And I don't think you're being patronizing or dehumanizing, quite the opposite, honestly. And her name is lovely. I've always like that flip on the term." Easton smiled.

"Flip?"

"Yeah, Nevaeh. Heaven. It's just Heaven in reverse. Not too uncommon. I have a cousin named Nevaeh. I've always thought it was a sweet reframing. Even if she's not the sweetest." Easton chuckled.

"Oh my god, I feel so stupid. Duh. Huh. Fascinating. It never occurred to me. I've never heard that name before, and always thought it was lovely, but had no idea." Samuel felt warm from the beer and the embarrassment.

"See, stick with me, Sam, you'll learn a few things. Black culture, Japanese culture. Culture in general. I'm just teeming with insight and translations." Easton laughed.

"So, you're black and Japanese, huh?" Samuel pushed the conversation away from his foolishness.

"Nope. Black on my father's and Filipino on my mother's side. My mom is second generation and never learned the language. She wasn't terribly interested in the culture or history, but I was a Japanese Studies minor—Social Services major—because I was always into Manga, embarrassingly enough. So, I know lots of things about Japanese culture. And Manga. And social sciences, actually. I'm riddled with oddities in all sorts of ways, Sam, my friend."

"Amazing." Samuel smiled, the butterflies in his stomach twirling.

"I am. You have no idea."

"I have a few." Samuel reached out across the table and pulled Easton's hand close. It was soft but firm, warm and just the right level of damp. Easton smiled into his beer, looking up at Samuel with kind eyes and a rugged smirk.

Their time at the bar flew by. Samuel didn't want the date to end, but he also didn't want to overstay his welcome. On any other date—*every* other date—he'd make a play to spend the night or invite Easton over for a romp and dump, but not tonight. He wanted to end things smartly, sweetly. He wanted to insure there would be a second date.

"It's not getting too late, but it might be time to think about heading home." Samuel smiled softly, working so hard not to sweat. On one hand, he wanted the night to last much longer, on the other he worried too much of a good thing could sour a lovely first date.

"I was thinking the same thing. I just didn't want to be the first person to say something." Easton shrugged, pulling back into the booth and sighing sweetly. His gaze lingered on Samuel softly, like he had a number of thoughts on his mind.

"Oh sure, make *me* do the dirty work." Samuel smirked playfully.

"Well, it's time you learn my style sooner or later, my dear Sam."

"Fine, then I get the pleasure and rights to ask you out on another date first." Samuel pointed at Easton, before quacking pulling back after realizing he was shaking a little. This was going well. So well. The joyful anxiety—a feeling that is so rare—was unfolding like warm laundry.

"To be fair, I think I was the first to drop the suggestion that this was the first of likely many dates to come." Easton leaned forward, raising an eyebrow.

"Oh damn. You're not wrong. I don't get to be the fun guy at all tonight." Samuel shook his head.

"Maybe ever." Easton volleyed back.

"Well, I'm up for testing that theory if you are?" Samuel returned smartly.

"I am." Easton gripped Samuel's hand tightly across the table. Time stood still for a moment as Samuel struggled with feeling like a kid on his first day at a new school, all sweaty palms and hopeful anxiety.

"So, when next, where?" Samuel stuttered a bit.

"In the spirit of good sportsmanship, I'll allow you to pick, Sam. I'm open most nights but Tuesdays and Wednesdays."

"Oh, a school night, huh? You don't want to waste any time." Samuel loved this banter, never wanting it to end. Easton narrowed his eyes, landing a coy smirk. Samuel took a final swig of his warmed beer.

"I can wait a week, if you feel like you have to blow a couple of guys off first." Easton shrugged, letting Samuel's hand drop dramatically on the table before leaning back playfully.

"Nice word play. Nope, my dance card is open. What about getting together on 14th street this coming Thursday for dinner at Dashbox? 7pm?" Samuel proposed.

"Love that place. Their mini burgers are stupid good. Yes, yes and yes." Easton sat up excitedly and pulled out his phone to make a note.

"With the mountain of crispy parmesan dusted onions on top? Why do you think I picked it? I'm not new to the city." Samuel blushed, wanting to show off he wasn't just a tourist in Easton's hometown.

Easton insisted on paying, since it was his home turf, with Samuel promising to get dinner the coming week.

"Can I walk you home?" Samuel asked, mildly interested to know where Samuel might live in the neighborhood.

"I was going to ask you if you wanted me to walk with you back to the Metro?" Easton smiled devilishly, arching his eyebrow high into the immediate inside joke.

"I think it's adorable you think I'm not calling a ride." Samuel bit his tongue. This night was oddly sweet, bubbly, and playful like a good prosecco. It was near perfect.

"I didn't convert you to the Metro lifestyle, huh?" Easton opened the door for Samuel out to the cooling street.

"Not even slightly." Samuel cooed, walking right past Easton's chiseled jaw.

"Fair enough. Call your ride but let me at least make sure you get in safely and off to home." Samuel ordered his car and within three far-too-short minutes, it swiftly arrived on site.

As the car sat ready to return Samuel home, the two men stood silent and unmoving for a few moments. Samuel didn't want the night to truly end, but he also didn't want to run the night into the ground. The night air hung around them cool and inviting. The streetlamps buzzed, throwing a yellow gleam across everything, including the lights dancing in both of their eyes.

"I know this wasn't a date-date, but is asking for a kiss a bit much?" Samuel asked.

"No. But not unless I get a hug, too," Easton immediately replied, sliding his thick arms around Samuel.

Easton's lips were soft, but firm, warm and wet. The kiss was too short, but it also felt like it lasted for minutes. The hug afterward grew a bit awkward, with Samuel feeling a bit randy from the beer and Easton's cheekbones and delicious backside. Samuel wondered if calling it a night was best, but also knew it felt right, even if it seemed so wrong. Samuel pulled Easton in for another quick hug. Easton laughed lightly, enjoying the flirty moment.

"I doubt your driver is loving this show."

"No, no, you're right. I know." Samuel backed up, weirdly offering his hand for a handshake.

"Oh, so we're also shaking hands now?"

"Yeah, um, good game?" Samuel winced, feeling stupid, but also completely out of whack emotionally. His feet turned to rocks, which was good because his head became a stringless balloon. He didn't want to get into the car, but he knew he needed to get home and let their date end sweetly.

"Good game, Sam." Easton shook Samuel's hand softly, before pulling it up and kissing it.

Samuel slipped into his ride, feeling a million different, wonderful, terrible, delightful things, and thanked the driver for his polite patience as his body thrummed with unspent energy.

Chapter Six

"How was dodgeball, Sammy boy?" Rachel asked dryly the next morning She leaned over the island in her poorly tied silk robe. "Did you knock the teeth out of any Congressional staffers or PAC leaders? I certainly hope the latter."

Samuel sat crossed-legged on the couch. His phone dinged with a notification–a sweet text from Easton—and he wished it was Thursday already. *Is it too forward to ask him to get coffee this Sunday morning?* He could just send another text back, wishing him well on whatever his day looked like. The idea of seeing anyone back to back normally sickened him, but not Easton.

"Samuel?" Rachel stood directly in front of Samuel, giving him an uncaring glance of more than just her irritation.

Samuel looked up and laughed then immediately covered his eyes again. "Oh god, Rach, put those away. Lord. You'll poke my eye out."

He heard the rumple of fabric before the couch sank next to him as she sat. As he opened his eyes again, she tried to move his arm so she could peek at his phone, the source of his distraction from her antics.

Samuel pulled back, embarrassed, hiding his phone from her view. "Stop."

"You stop. We have rules in this house, buddy." Her brow popped up and she made another grab for his phone.

"What rules?" he asked, keeping his arm extended so she couldn't reach it.

She let out a gusty sigh before folding her arms across her chest in frustration. "You can bury your face in your phone all you want, day or night, but not when I'm talking about politics, picking on you, or if we're trying to decide on where to get take-out. You just broke all three provisions."

"You didn't ask me where we should get breakfast."

She pointed a triumphant finger in his direction. "Ah-ha, you *did* hear me."

Samuel glanced at his phone again and sighed, unsure exactly what to say or if Rachel would make fun of him. Wanting to impress upon her that he wanted to have a moderately serious conversation, Samuel thought carefully about his next move.

He finally asked, "When you first met Phillipe, was it love at first sight?"

Rachel pulled all the way back, sinking a bit into the couch. She looked uncomfortable and a little irritated, but also far away.

Samuel began to backpaddle, realizing the topic might be a hard one for her. "I'm sorry. Never mind. It's none of my business..."

"No, I'll answer you." Rachel sat back up, truly pulling her robe tight. "Yes and no? I was a barista, and Phillipe was a high-profile lawyer in NYC. I've told you that, though. I honestly have no clue how many times I saw him or served him. He was so handsome, with his charming smile, dark curly hair, bushy eyebrows. No more than 5'8" but I've never been a tall-guy-girl. Anyway, all I saw endless handsome men getting coffee or tea. He didn't stand out, you know?"

Samuel was fully dialed in. He didn't know much about Phillipe, honestly. Rachel would often only casually reference him in places where they shared a moment—like a café or holiday—and then trail off. Sometimes, she'd mention him in a small fit of anger, because she couldn't remember a name, date or number, and she felt Phillipe likely would, solving this minor crisis more quickly. But he rarely seemed to be a subject matter open to casual conversation.

She fiddled with the belt on the robe as she explained. "I worked at that coffee shop for three months, so I likely served him off and on that long. One day, I was sweeping up, and he was there working on his laptop, and I accidently bumped into him. We struck up a little conversation. He was kind, engaging, sweet. He asked for my number. Actually, he mentioned that the first time I served him—a double hot Caffè Americano that I never recalled—he fell in love with *me*. But I didn't fall in love with him until that conversation. Which, I think is maybe fair to say was first-sight adjacent, because I honestly never really looked-looked at him until that day."

The room fell silent. Rachel was far away, deep in frustrated thought, like she'd just given up the cheat codes to a game she wanted to win.

"That's a very sweet story." Samuel said softly.

"Yep. Sure is." Rachel said. She slapped her legs with her open palms before rising and going into the kitchen to grab some coffee. He could almost see her shake off her anxieties and feelings, as if they were as easy to remove as the slippery robe.

He cared about her, though, and didn't want her to feel like she had to pretend not to hurt with him. "I'm sorry, I know you don't talk about him that much."

"Well, with you, sure." Rachel stirred sugar into her coffee with her finger.

"Oh." Samuel felt sucker-punched.

"I do with my mom, some of my old friends, my therapist. You know, the mental health tribe." She tried to laugh it off, but then her razor-sharp gaze focused on him. "Why did you want to know about him, anyway?"

Samuel tried to smear a little salve on his wounds. "You can tell me stuff, Rach. I don't want you to think your industry husband can't hear about your real husband."

"Aw, puppy. What is this really about? I love you, Sammy, but why would I tell a hotdog vender about a Michelin-star meal?" Rachel looked down quickly, realizing she went over the line for the sake of a funny, well-placed, truthful, but certainly stinging analogy.

"Fuck off. Nevermind." Samuel retreated, getting up off the couch and heading down the hallway into his room.

Rachel chased him down, but he figured it was just because she felt bad about being too harsh. "No, no, no. I actually don't mind talking about him. And it's sweet you asked, just out of character. Rare. That's all.

I'm sorry, that was a shitty thing for me to say. I know. I didn't mean it. I'm just being bitchy to be bitchy."

Samuel stood in his doorway, glaring at Rachel who was half-dressed and looking dressed down.

"No, you're not wrong. It's fine. I'm fine. I'm just tired. I need a nap." Samuel sighed, wishing he lived alone.

"Dude. You just got up. We both did. Let's figure out breakfast. Don't be a tool." Rachel pleaded, her voice going into a low purr. She liked to think she was playfully flirting, but the intent slipped under Samuel's skin.

"I'm not hungry" Samuel said dryly. The damage was done that morning. Rachel rolled her eyes and walked away back into the living room. Samuel felt stupid, embarrassed, completely out of his element. He *was* a hotdog vender. One of the nice ones—safe, fairly priced, lots of smart and inventive toppings, but he was just dolling out wieners to any willing customer. He wasn't invested in five-star meal material. *Until maybe now?* She wasn't wrong, but he wasn't ready to tell her about one little date that felt... different.

Samuel's phone rang. It was his mother.

"Hey, Mom."

"It's Sammy." His mom was talking to someone off the phone.

"Mom?"

"Give me a minute, I'm talking to *our* son," she said away from the phone again.

"Mom, can you hear me?" Samuel put his head in his free hand.

"Sammy?" His mother yelled into the phone.

"Yep. Hey, Mom." Samuel shook his head.

"Ok, good. I was just talking to... someone. The gardener."

"We don't have a gardener mom. I know it was Dad." Samuel laughed out loud at the madness of this exchange.

"No. We do have a gardener...well, a young man who rakes our leaves. Lives down the street. I want to say his name is Evan? Derek? I can't recall. He's maybe twelve." She scolded him like he had always known this insane fact.

"So, you were telling a pre-teen you were talking to 'our' son? A kid you can't even remember his name? This is some Maury-level stuff, mom." Samuel laughed again.

"Who?" She snapped in full irritation.

"Never mind. What did you need?" Samuel asked, shutting his bedroom door. Not even Rachel wanted to hear this painful exchange.

"Oh, listen to you. I don't *need* anything. I'm calling because I love you and wanted to see how you were and catch up." She said playfully, a clear indication she was lying.

Samuel shook his head. She'd just called last week. She never called twice in a handful of days without needing something, wanting something, or wanting to share some kind of news.

"I'm good. Great even. How are you? How is dad?" Samuel sighed openly, wanting to desperately signal he wasn't in the mood for a call.

"I told you he's not even here. I was talking to someone else." She shushed him, a sign she was consciously ignoring his tone.

"Right. Sure. But I mean, overall, in general existence, how is Dad? How are you?" Samuel perked up his voice a bit, knowing he was on the hook for this call no matter how he felt otherwise.

"Your father is fine. He sends his love, as always." She said curtly and quickly.

"Great. Sure." Samuel sighed again.

"And I'm fine. I mean, my hairdresser is apparently on vacation—whatever that means—so I'm having to work with some new girl tomorrow to get my roots touched up, which is never good news." Her normal, upright tone returned, unfortunately. Samuel rubbed his face with his available hand, daydreaming he could just throw his phone out the window and into the busy street below.

"Hairdressers are humans too, they take vacations like the rest of us." Samuel said dryly. He scanned the room for something sharp. Something he could fall on.

"I suppose you're likely right. Anyway, so I bumped into Michael again. Just yesterday, actually." She stopped talking. Samuel shook his head and sat down on his bed.

"Ah. Ok." This call's purpose was clear now. However, the usual sinking sensation that hit him whenever his mother mentioned Michael's name didn't happen, a remarkable enough occurrence that Samuel tilted his head to consider why.

His mother continued, "Yes, such a sweet boy. Always nice to see him. Anyway, he's getting married."

Samuel dropped his phone in his lap, as the room spun a bit.

"Sammy?" He could hear faintly below him while the world stood still for a moment. Samuel wasn't upset or happy, mad or grateful, just a bit numb. Unsure how to feel or if it even mattered, and moreover how to properly respond to his mother. Picking the phone back up, he let out a huge breath.

"That's nice to hear, Mom. Good for him. Good for Oliver. I'm happy for them." He was surprised to find the words were mostly true as he said them.

"That's what I said," she said.

"Well, good, we should be happy when good people find good things and make good choices." Samuel volleyed back.

"I agree. Which is why I told him it wouldn't be even slightly weird for you to attend the wedding. So sweet of him to ask, right?" She dropped casually. Which she always did, all the time. Casually spouting tectonic statements like it was asking to pass the salt. He should have seen this coming, but his fight with Rachel threw him off this morning.

"You told him what?" Samuel pushed out carefully. The room began to spin again, this time to the left.

"He seemed nervous to ask, but apparently Oliver feels the same. They felt you should be invited. They even invited me and your father. Such sweet boys." She sounded so proud of herself. Samuel could hear his teeth grinding a bit.

"He's inviting me? He *invited* me? I don't understand." Samuel asked more out loud to the Universe, rather than to his mother.

"Well, so, apparently the wedding is next weekend. Which was a shock to me, but it's not some shotgun thing. They've been planning this for about a year now. Anyway, he'd been debating inviting you, then bumped into me back-to-back, and he and Oliver thought it was a sign. And so, he's going to be calling you sometime today to formally invite you. Wanted to make sure you had a head's up. Such a sweet boy. Not sure your father and I will be going? But you should." She explained. He could literally hear her shit-eating grin through the phone.

"He's calling me. *Today*. To invite me to his wedding to Oliver, taking place next weekend." Samuel numbly repeated back.

"Yes, exactly. You got it." She replied bluntly.

"And you think I should go." He stood back up off the bed and began pacing around his room aimlessly. The implications here were a mile wide and a ocean deep. Of course, Michael invited him. And of course, his fiancé Oliver agreed. And of course, bumping into his mother seemed like some kind of divine sign. This was Michael at his absolute best, which is why Samuel felt so bad and so frustrated. Michael truly was the sweetest guy ever. And that sucked.

"Of course! We love Michael. You two were friends first, right?" She said, offering the most honest and rational perspective of the day.

"Yeah. We were. Are." Samuel stood still to think.

"Apparently, Sammy. And you don't have to go. You know that." Her voice softened. While she likely didn't feel bad to lay this at his feet, Samuel knew she wasn't a monster.

"No. I know. I just. I don't know, mom. I don't have any feelings for him. I truly don't. I'm happy for him. Oliver sounds great. This is all really very wonderful for them. But attending their wedding? *This* weekend? I mean. I don't know. It sounds insane when I say it out loud." Samuel looked out the window into the city. There were dozens of people walking below, going here or there, living their lives. DC was a constant reminder that life was always moving, always active, even if you were standing still. And maybe Michael's wedding was just another person walking past the window off to live their life and run their errands in the grand scheme of it all.

"Well, I told him, you would appreciate the personal call. And it seems you will. As for attending, you do what feels right. Michael asked if they should anticipate a plus-one, which was very sweet but funny." She laughed lightly. All the hair on Samuel's neck sprung to attention.

"Funny?" Samuel snapped.

"Well. Sammy. I mean. I know you live with that tense young lady you adore, but I assured Michael that you weren't *seeing* anyone serious. So, there was no reason to shell out for two meals just to make good on an act of generosity. Weddings are expensive, you know." She asserted like Samuel was five years old learning how manner worked at a fancy restaurant.

"Mom. What the hell?" Samuel snapped again.

"What? Am I mistaken? Are you *secretly* seeing someone? Are you keeping a beloved beau from me?" She said playfully, sounding confident in her shitty assertion.

Samuel let his arm drop, looking down at his phone once again, his finger hovering over the red button. He could tell her the internet went down, the lights went out, the bill was late. Without even really thinking, he pulled the phone back to his ear. Easton flashed into his mind unprompted. He was so hot. But so sweet. Hot enough to bring to an ex's wedding for sure, but also maybe too sweet to ask to do such a thing so quickly without seeming like a guy who only invited a hot guy to a wedding to make an ex feel a certain way. And yet.

"Well, actually, yeah. I am. I'm seeing someone, thank you very much." Samuel's brain and mouth were not fully yet in concert.

"Oh?" She mocked.

"Yeah. A really great guy. Newish, kinda. Not too new. Anyway, his name is Easton." It felt good to admit it out loud. And he wasn't entirely lying.

"Oh. Alright. Well, okay then. News to me, of course. He sounds lovely, I'm sure. Lots to talk about with Michael. A date for the wedding for you, how fun," she said, disarmed.

"Yep. He's smart and kind, and funny. Athletic. From DC, born and raised. And I'm sure available this weekend. So yeah, I'll be bringing him." Samuel replied, sounding confident but feeling anything but.

"Heston." She replied.

"Easton." Samuel volleyed back.

"Easton. Yes. Ok. Well good then. I look forward to meeting him next weekend." She said with an air of unfettered confidence.

"What? I thought you and dad weren't going to Michael's wedding?" Samuel's brain glitched a bit. Taking Easton was one thing, meeting his terrifying parents too was another.

"We're not. But I'll make up the nice guest room for you two. I'll meet him the night before or for a meal before you both head back to DC, I'm sure. We'll sort that out." She said mindlessly, as if this was all normal and expected and warranted.

"Oh my god. We're *not* staying with you two." Samuel laughed.

"Fine, we can meet you at the hotel for a meal. Whatever seems best. The Sheraton apparently has a very nice restaurant. Lovely environment to meet Christian." She replied far too casually for Samuel's liking.

"Easton, mom. *Easton.*" Samuel shook his head, hearing the return of his grinding teeth.

"Easton, yes. I'll need to write that down. Like the direction on a compass? East?" She asked.

"Yep. That's the one." Samuel teeth were so tight, he worried he'd have a mouth full of powder if he didn't get off the phone soon.

"Good, then. Excited to see you boys this weekend. For Michael's wedding. Wonderful."

"Yep. Wonderful indeed. I'll text with details later in the week."

"Good. Love you. Dad sends his love, too." She remarked, clearly pulling back from the phone.

"I send mine right back." Samuel said hanging up. He laid back to stare at the ceiling for a while, calmly waiting for the phone call from Michael.

Chapter Seven

Samuel arrived early to Dashbox before being quickly seated by the chipper hostess ahead of Easton arriving.

The waitress smiled. "Can I get you something to drink to get started?"

"Ah, wine. No, water. No, wine. Anything. Chardonnay," Samuel stammered, wishing Easton was already present, but grateful to be alone for a moment longer to collect this thoughts.

The call with Michael went well. As always, and due to his nature, he was upbeat and direct in that he and Oliver *both* would welcome and appreciate his and a guest's attendance at their wedding and reception. Michael explained that Oliver was hesitant at first—as anyone might be when suggesting a prior fiancé's boyfriend attend their wedding—but like so many things involving Michael, he was just so earnest, good-hearted, and joyful about everything and everyone in his life. Even Samuel and his new boyfriend.

Although, it didn't slip past Samuel that Michael seemed fairly relieved at the request of bringing Easton as a date. Maybe it would quell any final concerns of Oliver's, or maybe even Michael had some lingering doubts, but the mere mention of Easton set the remainder of the casual conversation into a more calming and lighthearted tone.

"I'm glad you're coming, Sam. I want the people I cherish to celebrate with me."

"I'm honored you invited me, Michael."

"Aw, you big formal goof, of course you're invited. We were friends before anything else. And friends we remain, right?"

"Right."

From across the room, Samuel spotted Easton. He lit up the room with his smile, his cheekbones enjoying a casual battle for attention with his dimples. He wore a tight navy polo and khaki pants with a brown belt and loafers. He was stunning, perfect. Samuel stood up and waved him over to their table.

"Wow, you got seated already? On a Thursday? How early did you have to get here?" Easton kissed Samuel on the cheek before taking a seat.

"Just crazy timing, I've only been here for a few minutes. You look great. Nice to see you clean up well."

Easton sat down and sighed, his smile brightened, his eyes twinkled with the tea candle on the table. "You look really nice, too. This was a long week."

"Agreed. Work was crazy for you?"

"No. Just waiting for tonight." They both blushed.

Samuel reached out and took Easton's hand in his, rubbing his thumb across his firm, soft knuckles. The room stood still, lit by candles and heartbeats and hope. "Same."

They both ordered drinks and entrees, casually chatted about their respective weeks. Samuel didn't even know where to begin with his opportunity-meets-dilemma, so he was glad Easton kept the conversation light and easy. Finally, the subject arrived organically on its own with no place else to run.

Easton waved a fork as he said, "I meant to text you about this during the week and kept forgetting—a good friend of mine is directing a play this weekend at the Fluffy Antelope Theater. I could get us really good tickets, if you wanted to go?"

"This weekend only?" Samuel frowned, hoping it was true.

Easton shook his head. "No, this Saturday is the opening. I believe the show runs for three to four weeks, actually, so we could go another time, if you wanted, instead."

"Um. Maybe. Yeah. No, yeah." Samuel stammered.

Easton's brow furrowed as he carefully considered Samuel's face. "Or we could skip it altogether. Do something else? I know not everyone likes theater, local theater, even."

Samuel reached for his hand. "No. Sorry. Yes, we should go. I'm even up for this weekend, because I'm sure attending the opening is a big deal for you. A huge deal for your close friend."

Easton appeared relieved and he gave Samuel's fingers a squeeze before grabbing his glass for a long sip of water. "Ha. Honestly, she'll likely never even notice us. Big, crazy night for her, but I like the idea of supporting her. We can pick another weekend. Do something else instead."

Samuel smiled, sipping his drink. "Yeah. No. I mean, I'd hate for her to look out, not see you. Opening night and all. But you could twist my arm. We could make this weekend work. Absolutely."

"Twist your arm, huh? So, do you want to go or not?" Easton cocked his head and drew up his eyebrow. Samuel could tell Easton knew something was up.

"No, yeah. I mean, I don't hate theater. Sorry if I'm giving off that impression." Samuel stumbled around his thoughts verbally, not sure how to address the elephant tramping around in his brain.

"I honestly can't tell what impression you're trying to give, Sam." Easton laughed.

"Right. No, sorry. You're right. I might have a thing—this weekend—and you're invited, too, actually. Funny enough. But at the same time, I'm not sure if I even want to go. Or if *you'd* even want to go. Or if we should go at all. In the first place. You know?" Samuel laughed anxiously, knowing full well he sounded insane.

"Not really no." Easton sobered a bit, his eyes narrowing in amused, but still sheer confusion.

Samuel realized he might be making it sound far worse than he meant to, worried Easton would read too much into his hesitation if he couldn't find the right words to be just open and honest and transparent. He wasn't sure if he wanted to go to Michael and Oliver's wedding, but if he did, he loved the idea of going with Easton. However, they had only known one another for a few days. And he liked Easton. But an ex's wedding? That's on another level.

"You must think I'm nuts, but it's a wedding. This weekend, actually. Back in my hometown in Indiana." Samuel admitted, feeling a much-needed rush of air finally fill his lungs.

"Ok." Easton said slowly.

"And I'm invited—just got invited. In fact, we're both invited, as insane as that sounds." Samuel tried to explain. Poorly.

"Ok." Easton smirked, leaning forward while crossing his arms over the table.

"But we barely know each other. Which isn't a problem. I like you, Easton. I just don't want you think I'm insane. You know?"

"I don't think you're insane. A bit neurotic, maybe. But I'm not uninterested." Easton smiled kindly, the kind when you find the sweetest dog you had hoped to adopt on the first trip to a shelter. The room was electric joy.

"No, fair enough. But. Well. Technically, there's more." Samuel closed one eye tight, as if he expected to be tackled.

"Is it *your* wedding, Sam?" Easton fluttered his eyes playfully and chuckled lightly. Samuel thought it was almost unfair how handsome this guy was considering how sweet and funny he was being about something so awkward.

"No. No, that would be one hell of a twist, right? No, but it's in the ballpark, maybe. It's my ex's wedding. From several years ago, to a wonderful man. They're both wonderful men, Michael and Oliver. Michael being the ex. Too wonderful, maybe, inviting me, essentially us, to their wedding." Samuel's face felt hot, the room felt stuffy. Saying this out loud was weird. But hoping for a kind, thoughtful response felt like a special kind of torture.

"Are you two close? This seems fairly last minute." Easton asked, his eyes darting side to side a bit, while taking in all of the information.

"No, exactly. I had no idea. And no, we're not close exactly, but we've always stayed friendly. Michael is a very sweet, goofy, genuine guy. I hear Oliver, his fiancé, is great. It's a small town. He and my mother bump into one another fairly often. Several times recently, and Michael apparently saw it as a sign he should invite me, I guess. Last minute. It's a very Michael thing to do, actually. In a good way." Samuel felt a sigh of relief that Easton had real questions and moreover, wasn't running for the door.

"And you get a plus one?" Samuel playfully walked his fingers across the table toward Samuel. But it only made Samuel feel like maybe he needed to truly explain himself more, even if it meant making things a touch more awkward.

"Um. No. Well, not exactly. At first."

"Sam..." Easton pulled his hand back slightly and frowned.

"No, sorry. Let me try and explain. I'm not close with my mom. I mean, we talk frequently enough I suppose, but I don't share much with her about my personal life. Ever. She's a handful, demanding, frustrating. Invasive as hell. Michael was kind enough to ask her if I was—would—bring someone. Like I said, such a nice guy, Michael. And then, because she wouldn't know better, told him flatly said I wouldn't. Because I don't tell her anything. Ever."

"Ah." Easton giggled, drinking his wine with a bit more obvious enthusiasm as he took in these details.

"Right. It all caught me off guard, Easton. I'm sorry. So, I told her I did have a date. Because maybe I do? You don't have to go. I don't even know if I want to go. I know we barely know each other. I've never even met Oliver. Maybe this whole thing is a huge mistake. I feel like this is the start of a chaotic rom-com you didn't sign-up for, you know?" Samuel pleaded, feeling honest, but also hoping being so honest would win him some much desired points.

"I like rom-coms, for the record." Easton reached across the table, gripping Samuel's hand tightly. The butterflies made a few barrel-rolls in response.

"You do, huh?" Samuel's pulse raced for a new reason. He hoped for such a response, but never dreamed he'd get one.

"Yep. I weirdly do," Easton said softly, the candlelight dancing in the pools of his dark, dreamy eyes.

"So, then... we're going, I guess?" Samuel chuckled, still slightly perplexed by the entire series of events that had unfolded in the past few days.

Easton's sweet gaze warmed Samuel's icy nerves. "I can't see why not. I mean, if we're being honest with each other, I pushed everything I would have been doing this weekend to make sure I could hopefully snag another date with you. I'm technically wide open."

"Ok. Well, I'm excited. Mostly. Nervous? Maybe even stupid. But alright, let's do this. What's the worst that could happen?" Samuel said, finally feeling hungry enough to eat.

"Hey now, Sam. Don't tempt fate with a question like that. You're not wrong that this is rom-com territory. Any number of terrible things could happen." Easton laughed loudly, cutting into his steak.

They both laughed over their entrees. By the time they finished a shared bruleed lemon tart at the end of the date, the plans were set. Samuel would pick Easton up around noon after renting an SUV, giving them about eight hours on the road west, before checking into their hotel room for the night. The wedding was scheduled for early afternoon on Saturday.

The long road trip was filled with salty snacks, sweet drinks, and slightly awkward banter. Confined to a car together, both men realized they took the time to get to know each other. While the several hours on the road was ripe with discovery, it was also a veritable powder keg of potential chaos.

"Speed round time. Do you have any siblings?" Easton asked, crunching on some peanut-butter pretzels.

"Only child. You?" Samuel volleyed back.

"One older sister, Avalon. She and I aren't really that close, however. It's complicated." Easton replied quickly.

"Sorry," Samuel responded, but he understood. His relationship with his family could also be described best as complicated.

"No, nothing to be sorry about..." Easton trailed off. The car grew a bit quiet through much of the drive. It wasn't painful, but it wasn't pleasant either.

"So, I'll be meeting your parents, huh?" Easton asked while they stopped for gas.

"No. Maybe. Depends. I'm not sure, actually. But probably not." Samuel expressed in a steam of uneasy consciousness.

"Okay." Easton replied meekly.

"It's not about you. Well, not entirely." Samuel was lost in a dozen complex thoughts.

"Alright." Easton seemed to retreat a bit while stretching his legs.

"No, sorry. I'm sorry. My parents are. They're..." Samuel called over the car, wishing Easton was facing him so he could see that he didn't mean anything personal. In an alternative universe, he'd love to introduce someone like Easton to a pair of loving parents. But this was their world and these parents.

"We don't have to talk about this, I promise." Easton got back into the car and bucked in, glancing out the window quietly. He poked his finger in the edge of the car and the window like he was feeling for something.

"No. Shit. Sorry, I feel like I'm only leaving all this room for endless speculation. I told you a bit about my mom. Ok, so, and I don't really talk to my dad. Like, at all. Or he doesn't really talk to me, I guess. Mostly the gay thing these days, but also, we just never really gelled as humans? If that makes sense. All my life I never felt like he saw me as me, only as something that I was doing weird or wrong or backwards." Samuel spilled out, not feeling like he was being clear enough, but still hoping it would resonate a little with Easton.

Easton turned back and softly frowned at Samuel, "That sucks. I'm sorry. I get it."

"Yeah. And then my mom? Like I said, she's a handful. In some ways she over-compensates for him, for them. In other ways, she's effortlessly herself, but in often unpleasant ways. She's a bit... elitist and racist? Maybe? But not in some terrible, Nazi-kind-of-way, but in that almost worse casual-over-coffee-kind-of-way." Samuel sighed as he drove, wishing the were driving anywhere else but to his hometown. He didn't even really know Easton and already he wanted something better for him too, when it came to his own parents.

"Yikes." Easton chuckled, putting his hand on top of Samuels. The car felt instantly warmer.

"Yeah, exactly. So, will we see my parents? I kind of hope not. I have absolutely no plans, trust me. But could we? Yeah, who knows. It's a small town." Samuel let out a long, careful sigh, feeling lost in his own thoughts, but grateful that Easton didn't seem as far away.

"I get it. It's all ok." Easton gripped Samuel's hand tightly.

"It's not, Easton. That's the thing. So, what about yours?" Samuel wanted to change the subject.

"My what?" Easton asked, confused.

"Parents." Samuel chuckled in response.

"Ah. Right. Them. I guess it's a natural question, after talking about yours." Easton replied, pulling his hand back into his lap. Easton blew out a frustrated breath. "I mean, what more is there to say from what I told you at the bar, I guess? At the end of the day, I don't talk to either of them. I haven't for almost twenty years. I was mainly raised by Auntie Regina, for the most part."

Samuel's smile crept back. "Oh. So that *was* your bedroom?"

Easton's whole body stiffened. He pulled his arms up and crossed them, remaining quiet for a moment. Outside the car the air was hot, but inside it instantly turned to ice.

Easton said carefully, "Um. Yeah. I mean, she did her best. She was strict, but kind. She saw *me*, you know? She got me. And ultimately, she raised me. It's complicated."

"Did she raise your sister?" Samuel asked, wishing Easton would share more about himself freely. He could tell there were lots of walls sheltering a real conversation.

"No. Just me." Easton replied with a soft shrug.

The car fell silent again. Samuel wasn't sure what was wrong, but Easton's tone was far-away, flat. His gaze remained locked outside the passenger window, watching the side of the road whipping by at lightspeed.

"Sorry." Samuel finally said quietly, the butterflies in his stomach suspended in flight. Easton turned to him and frowned softly. His deep brown eyes were competing with Samuel carefully watching the road more closely.

"There is nothing to be sorry about, Sam. I had a good childhood for the most part. Auntie did her best. I did mine. And all in all, everything worked out alright. Truly." Easton reached over and put his hand on Samuel's, resting on the center console as if to try to bring a bit of warmth to the ride.

By the time they had arrived at the hotel, both men were tired, hungry, and feeling a little emotionally empty, but hopeful. Which was odd given how little either shared, both trying so hard to dodge deeper topics and still empathize blindly. They checked into the massive hotel, dropped off their bags, and headed down to the hotel restaurant to grab some real food and stiff drinks. The entire place was packed—the parking lot, hotel, restaurant. After a few drinks and some delicious but over-salted food shared over careful, cautious conversation, the two retreated back to their room to unwind.

"Is it weird, being back?" Easton asked, pulling out some sleep pants and a NUUDE sage t-shirt from his overnight bag.

Samuel shrugged. "Yes and no? I'm glad we came mostly. Michael was a nice guy, good boyfriend. Just not the right one for me."

Easton slipped into the bathroom to change and wash his face.

"Are you taking a shower?" Samuel cooed through the door, the two drinks he'd had hitting him nicely a little below the belt.

"No. Why?" Easton asked, sounding anxious from the other side.

Samuel walked his fingertips across the door. "Well, we could if you wanted. Wash the stink of the drive off. Soap each other up?"

"Um. No. I'm good. Thanks," Easton sounded chipper, but curt.

Opening the bathroom door to the rest of the room, Easton paused, eyes wide, when he saw Samuel stripped down to his boxer briefs, smiling like a delighted devil, hard as a rock.

"We could shower later instead then." Samuel tugged at this balls.

"Um. Oh. Wow. Hey there, Sam. Look at you. Handsome and mostly naked." Easton quickly slipped by in his sleep pants and t-shirt, walking swiftly toward the king bed. He sat and hugged a king-size pillow in his lap. "I'm tired. Really tired. Aren't you kind of tired, Sam?"

Samuel smiled. "Exhausted, but not *so* exhausted, you know?"

"I do know. I do. But not tonight. Okay? Is that alright? If we wait?"

Samuel sobered a bit at the foot of the bed, feeling a little stupid, but also frustrated. He didn't realize he'd missed a telling cue somewhere. This entire adventure seemed so painfully off-kilter, like a drunk ballerina trying to impress an unwilling crowd.

"No. Yeah. Of course. Sorry. I just thought. You know what, doesn't matter." Samuel retreated into the bathroom to scold himself in the mirror and cool off a little.

After a few moments of silence, Easton's voice came through the bathroom door. "You don't have to apologize, Sam. I'm sorry. I just. I just can't. Yet. Tonight. I just can't yet, tonight. You know? I hope that's ok?"

Samuel looked himself in the mirror in silence. His reflection stared back, looking tired and a little bloated. He didn't feel sexy, but he was certainly horny.

And a little sad. Extremely tired. It *was* alright, but it didn't feel good to be rejected. For a brief moment again, he wished he came alone. He could've picked some poor guy out of the restaurant, had his way, and then pushed him out the door before getting ready for the wedding. *The good ole days.*

The thought made him laugh, since it had only been about a week since the 'good ole days.' *So why does it feel like so much longer?* Easton was worth waiting for; he knew it. But it didn't change feeling stupid about the whole thing. Rachel would find all of it so funny—she'd cut the tension with a biting comment. Splashing some cold water on his face and scolding his dick to stand down for the night, Samuel exited the bathroom. Easton still sat on the bed, pillow in his lap, looking at his phone.

"I'm sorry, too. It's fine. Of course, it's fine. I'm just a horndog. You're handsome. This is a hotel. You know how this stuff goes. My junk has a mind of its own, as I'm sure yours does, too."

Easton's eyes narrowed as he pulled his phone a bit closer before putting it back down.

"Yeah. Exactly. Sure."

Samuel teased, "Think nothing of it. I mean it, okay? I can sleep next to you and keep my hands to myself. My parents are monsters, but they absolutely didn't raise one."

"Thanks. And I promise, it's not you." Easton rolled away from Samuel, clutching his pillow tightly.

"I get it. You don't have to explain yourself. I swear." Samuel said softly.

"Okay. Thanks."

Both men slid into their respective sides of the bed and turned off the lights. The room, dark, smelling fresh and cool, allowed a slightly inebriated Samuel to fall asleep quickly.

Chapter Eight

Samuel still struggled to find something to say over breakfast, and Easton wasn't talking, either. While neither was truly hungover, Samuel felt so, and Easton looked the same. Easton picked over his goat cheese and mushroom omelet, while Samuel instantly regretted ordering pancakes on a day when he had to wear a well-tailored suit. It was a post-blackout favorite and certainly fit his mood.

"How did you sleep?" Easton asked, breaking the silence.

"Fine. I'm a bit dehydrated. Pillows were too soft, but overall fine. You?"

"Alright." Easton nodded, still needling his omelet, but not really eating it.

The waitress came over and refilled both of their coffee mugs to the brim without asking or leaving room for any additions. The room hung still. Samuel cautiously scanned the room for anyone he knew from town, but thankfully he didn't identify anyone. He wasn't in the mood to make introductions or pretend things weren't awkward.

"I feel like all I do is apologize anymore, but I'm sorry if you're likely regretting inviting me out there, to the wedding." Easton said quietly, finally taking a bite of his breakfast.

"What? No. Easton, no. Not at all. Honestly, I've been assuming you wished I hadn't invited you. I'm glad you're here. I'm sorry about last night. I was drunk. You're handsome. I was horny. It got weird. I should have asked, or we could have talked first. I don't know. I just hope you're not mad at me." Samuel stirred sugar into his coffee, feeling like some kind of jerk or bully.

"I'm not mad at all. I get it. You're handsome too. I'm often horny myself. I'm just not ready. Yet. That's all." Easton said softly. Samuel could tell he was searching for a little eye contact but Samuel wasn't ready to feel that vulnerable until his 2nd cup of coffee.

"I respect that." Samuel nodded, taking massive swig of his coffee and looking cautiously over the mug's brim at Easton. He was hunched over a bit and his eyes looked tired.

"Thanks." Easton smiled with pursed lips and folded hands.

While they both felt a bit better, the tension still oddly lingered. They had several hours to kill before the wedding, so Samuel suggested a short little drive to the local zoo. Easton agreed but seemed unenthusiastic.

Walking solemnly out of the restaurant, both men all but completely crashed into Michael and Oliver entering the lobby.

"Sam!" Michael cheered with true surprise and enthusiasm.

"Michael." Samuel replied, a bit taken back and far less enthusiastic.

They hugged briefly, but long enough for Samuel to smell clay, paint, and pine on Michael. Smells he knew well. Smells that used to simultaneously excite and irritate Samuel. But now, something that felt like coming home but didn't elicit a lick of homesickness. It was comforting, but also a revelation.

Michael got to introductions. "Sam, I'm so so so glad you came. Crazy. So cool. So good. Yay. Sam, this is Oliver. Oliver, this is Sam."

Oliver shook his hand. "It's really nice to meet you, Sam. I've heard nothing but good stuff from Mikey. We're both really grateful you took us up on the invitation." Oliver was older, shorter, stocky. Red hair and beard. Grip like a vice and hands that felt rough. It would have been sexy if it wasn't his ex's fiancé. He had a kind, genuine smile. His overalls and artsy flannel shirt, where the only dead give-away that he and Michael had anything in common. Samuel thought he was a lovely match for Michael.

He genuinely meant it when he said, "It's really nice to meet you, Oliver. And thank you, it was very kind to even extend the invitation. I'm really happy for you both, and for Michael."

Oliver chuckled. "Ha. '*Michael*, you were right baby, listen to him. So formal. Love it."

Samuel stiffened a bit, shooting Michael a glance and automatically wondering what else he'd shared. Without missing a beat, though, he said, "And this is my date, Easton."

Michael reached right out and hugged Easton tightly. Oliver shook his hand kindly.

"It's really wonderful to meet Sam's new guy. I had no idea. This is wonderful. I'm so grateful you're both here. You just made my day!" Michael beamed.

"I sure hope not. It's your wedding day, after all," Samuel said with a laugh.

"No, it did. It does! I'm happy for us. You found Easton. I'm marrying Oliver. We did well, Sam. I'm excited for us." Michael was all toothy grin and beaming eyes. He really was thrilled for everyone. *Of course he would be, he's that kind of guy.*

Right as Samuel was filled with warm thoughts about him, Michael said, "Did you plan any time to visit your parents? If you do, please thank your mom again for me. She's a dear."

Samuel sputtered, "I like to think of her as more the road-kill type. Or maybe the offending car. Ha. But No. No plans for that. I wouldn't dare torture poor Easton that way."

Michael frowned. "Aw, she's not that bad, Sam. A bit rough around the edges, sure. And your dad will come around someday. They always do."

"Not mine, I don't think, Michael." Samuel nodded, frowning at Michael with years' worth of history between them.

"Not all parents, unfortunately." Easton agreed, slipping his hand into Samuels.

"Have faith, gents." Oliver offered optimistically with a kind wink.

Samuel decided it was time someone changed the subject. "Enough depressing parental nonsense. You kids are getting married! What are you doing here? Did you stay the night?"

Michael and Oliver explained how they had just checked in and were going to grab some tea before heading out to get ready for the day. All four men hugged again and congratulated each other over their various circumstances before excitedly promising to see each other in a few short hours, heading on their separate ways.

The zoo was packed, but a beautiful, entertaining distraction. Samuel and Easton walked the grounds holding hands and keeping fairly quiet. Samuel felt like he was somehow inconveniencing Easton, while simultaneously feeling strongly that if it were actually true, he would die inside a little. After a few brief hours of naming monkeys, getting lost in the aquarium, and inhaling far too much cotton candy, they were already heading back to the hotel to get changed for the wedding.

The wedding was gorgeous, simple, but inspired. They'd decided to forgo a traditional wedding party and stood before their friends, family, witnesses, and God to share vows in front of a teary-eyed lesbian episcopal pastor with multi-colored hair. She led a few prayers before calling them husbands and asking them to kiss in front of everyone to signify their union.

Between the wedding and reception to make good on few hours in-between, Samuel drove Easton around his hometown, pointing out various memories, changes, and trappings, while gleefully storytelling on autopilot about his childhood experiences, teenage madness, and early twenties inspirations. Easton seemed amused, but fully distracted. Samuel could tell things were still off between them, but he didn't know how to fix the growing and unfortunate dynamics.

By the time the reception began, Samuel felt a bit burned out from dodging so many unspoken emotional and conversational bullets, scared he'd screwed everything up, and unsure how to articulate his remorse or how to ask for forgiveness. He wondered if he should offer to get Easton his own room, or at least switch to a room with two queen beds.

At the reception, he ran out of things to pretend to talk about. He focused on exchanging names and pleasantries with the strangers sharing their table, which was clearly a misfit-toy menagerie filled with prior co-workers, random connections, and third cousins. It felt an appropriate placement as both a former boyfriend of one of the grooms, and someone who had only been invited five days prior.

Once dinner was being served, Samuel realized he hadn't spoken to Easton for a solid half an hour or more. The music and dancing had also begun. With the lights dimmed a bit and the room swelling with thumping bass, guests swaying, and festive frivolities, Samuel wondered if he should suggest they retire to their room early, so he could ask Easton in the quieter lobby if he wanted a different or separate room. The day was clearly over, and Samuel wasn't personally interested in dancing or visiting with anyone.

Watching a group of Michael's young nieces dance chaotically uneven circles while dressed in little fancy outfits, Samuel saw a chance to strike up a new, casual conversation.

"Did you ever wear a dress, like for drag, or as a kid?"

Easton tensed up unexpectedly. Samuel bristled in response, feeling like this might be the final straw in a long few days of unexpected and unnecessary tension.

"Um. Ha. Yeah. Well, I did, actually. When I was young. All the time." Easton remarked slowly, turning around with a funny smile. It was the first time Samuel had seen Easton smile since the giraffes.

"Oh really? You were one of *those* gay kids, huh?" Samuel laughed awkwardly, still feeling on edge and a bit confused, but grateful they were talking a little again.

"Nope. I wasn't a gay kid at all, in fact. I wasn't technically 'gay' until more recently." Easton locked eyes with a confused Samuel and stopped speaking. The room narrowed between the two of them. Easton's eyes bounced back and forth to Samuels, leaving Samuel knowing he wasn't fully grasping something being shared.

"I'm not following." Samuel said carefully, unsure if he heard Easton correctly over the music.

"No, I know. I'm sorry. Why would you? How could you, I guess." Easton shook his head sadly before smiling again like he was about to tell a sad child their dog just went to live on The Big Farm.

"Are you okay? Are *we*?" The room uncomfortably spun around Samuel as he leaned closer to Easton. "Because I am really sorry about last night. I'm sorry if you're hating all of this. I'm sorry I dragged you all over my neighborhood. I feel terrible. I hate that we're not okay. Can I do something to fix it? Did I do something else wrong?"

Easton drew in a tight breath. "No. Not all, Sam. But you *might*. And it's freaking me out. And so, I'm doing my best, because I *really* don't want you to. I really like you, Sam. But I've been in my head all day. All week. Since I met you honestly. And you were right when you invited me over dinner in the first place—we barely know each other."

"No, I know, but what do you mean? Don't want me to do what? You're kind of freaking me out, Easton."

Easton sat up and looked around the room a little. Samuel felt the room go silent, like tinnitus, just a single stream of sound that sounded like nothing and everything combined. Easton, shifted forward in his seat, so he was at close to Samuel as possible without touching and leaned in carefully. He looked sad but confident. His eyes were soft but his jaw was firm. There was a line of sweat forming at his temples.

"I'm trans, Sam."

Like a game of Tetris, all the pieces of the week fell together at once in a clean, clear line for Samuel. The music resumed and the room stopped spinning. While there was a sense of sudden relief, a million questions began to leak out between the pieces.

"Oh. Um. Okay. Okay." Samuel sputtered out, unsure what to say next or how to best express himself in the intimate immediacy.

"*Are* you ok? Are we ok? Am I?" Easton asked, pulling back a bit and scanning the room a little bit again. The dew on this temples grew into droplets.

"Yeah. Yes. Absolutely. I mean, you could have. I don't know..." Samuel kept sputtering, still feeling his brain and mouth forgetting how to double-Dutch.

"Told you sooner." Easton cut him off with a cool look in his eyes. He pulled his chair back a bit away.

"Wait. No, sorry. Not like that. Maybe. I mean..." Samuel stammered. His throat tightening while his mind pushed for expansion.

"So you wouldn't have had to bring me to this wedding?" Easton seemed so prepared for fallout, he didn't even notice Samuel's rising panic.

"Wait. Easton, no. That's not what I meant. That's not it at all. Hold on." Samuel leapt a bit forward out of his chair to plead with Easton, pushing Easton to stand up, walking behind his chair and holding on to the back until his knuckles went white while facing Samuel. The two men shared pleading, panicked looks for every different, contrasting reasons. The music in the room kicked into high gear and a whole new decibel as the dance floor beyond them swelled and bounced.

"You don't get it. There isn't always a good time to tell people, Sam. I wish there were. You tell people too soon and they usually never give you a chance – or worse, they treat you like a secret vacation or mistake. Tell them too late and it gets bad Sam. Acting like you tricked them, or worse, like I lied." Easton yelled over his chair and the deafening music.

"Okay." Samuel yelled back and put his hand on Easton's hand. He knew it wasn't his time to talk yet. The best thing he could do was stand still, make constant eye-contact, listen and hear.

The tension practically dripped off Easton as he continued, "But it's *not* a trick. I'm not trying to hurt you. I'm just trying to live my life. As a man. Because I'm a man. A 'trans man' but a man, nonetheless. It's not like I have an STD you can catch. It's not like I'm a monster or a murderer or something. And it's not like I'm not who I say who I am. Who I know I am. *What* I am."

Samuel smiled softly and gripped his hand harder. "Ok, Easton. I understand. I swear."

"Because I *like* who I am." Easton dropped his head and put his other hand on top of Samuel's hand on his own, standing silent in the noise.

Samuel looked around the room filled with loud, happy, dancing, drinking people and children running amuck. He knew so many of them—Michael's friends, family and loved ones, some people he'd known for over a decade, in some cases. But there was an even larger group of people he didn't know at all—likely Oliver's friends, family, and loved ones. He realized there was a third group he'd never be able to identify, a diverse mixture of those in the room who were loved by and beloved to Michael and Oliver, *together*. People they mutually knew, spend time with, or met over the past three years.

Samuel turned back to look at Easton, still standing, slumped over his chair a bit. He looked like he was almost praying. He'd only known him for a week. *One week.* What did that add up to? When was the right time to tell someone something like *I'm trans*? He was an amazing man. He was the whole package.

And Samuel knew he had real feelings for Easton. Feelings unlike ever before. Easton was handsome, kind, funny, charming, witty, smart, and sweet. And so many *other* things he didn't know yet, things that excited and intrigued Samuel. They didn't even know anyone mutually yet. But there was so much there to consider, explore, and become excited about. Samuel felt sick and splendid, erratic and ecstatic—all at the same time. And he liked it.

"Easton?" Samuel leaned over closely pulling his nervous lips toward Easton's ear. "In case it's not clear, I like who you are. I didn't know all of this, but I invited *you* here. All of you."

Easton finally looked up, his expression unsure and painfully hopeful. The music finally pulled back as a ballad was being played and the dancefloor melted into dozens of couples of all races, ages, and genders paired off to dance arm in arm or warm embrace.

Samuel continued just as loud as he had spoken over the raging music, "I like you a lot, Easton. But just so I'm clear on the finer details, you've *never* murdered anyone?"

"What?" Easton chuckled looking around anxiously, shushing Samuel. He still seemed a bit unsure, but hope blossomed beautifully in his gorgeous eyes.

Samuel shrugged playfully, his eyes going wild. "Because you're kind of putting me on the spot, Easton. I don't have an STD, either—at least not anymore, don't ask—and I haven't technically murdered anyone dead, anyway. I mean, I *am,* however a deadly orator and once crushed the soul of a kid I faced at a high school Model U.N. debate so badly, rumor had it he not only quit the team, but also transferred schools from the shame."

"Oh my god, Sam. Why are you screaming? You're insane." Easton laughed, pulling him closely, face to face. Samuel could smell Easton. Leather, musk, and just a hint of wildflowers. It was a smell he'd been struggling to identify over the past few weeks but had come to crave every time he took a deep breath. It felt like the future. It sent shivers down his fiery back. It was a place he'd like to call home.

Samuel leaned in so their eyebrows almost danced together to the next ballad. "I hope you do, because we all have secrets, or maybe truths that aren't so obvious or evident. And I want you to know that, while I have a million questions, I hope I'll have the chance to not only ask them and learn about the answers, but that over time, you'll have a million for me, too, and will want to hear about me. Because I like you very much. *You*, Easton. Whoever you unfold to be as we get to know each other. Because I see you. All of you. And I like what I see. I like who you are. Very much."

"Damn man." Easton pulled back and smiled brightly. His posture eased into something more comfortable, more normal.

Samuel raised a brow. "I told you I was a great orator."

"I mean, you seem fine, I guess." Easton smirked, pulling back a bit and put his hand out and nodded for Samuel to take it.

"I don't dance." Samuel was taken back.

"I don't either. I hoped to lead you someplace more private, maybe." Easton purred.

Samuel's grin grew. "Now *that* I do."

Easton chuckled but shared a knowing grin. "Don't get ahead of yourself, there, buddy."

Samuel took Easton's hand. They quickly slipped out of the busy reception and into lobby, slightly skipping as they sped down the long hallway.

Once at the door of their room, Easton turned around swiftly, putting his hand on Samuel's chest. Theair was full of sparks of colorful lightning.

"Are you sure you want to do this?" Samuel asked, putting his hand on Easton's.

"Yes. Are you?" Easton said quietly, his eyes searching Samuel's.

"Yeah. Yes." Samuel said with growing confidence and swelling pants.

"Then yes. I do, too. Very much." Easton replied softly.

Sliding into the room, both men started taking off their jackets and dress shirts in a passionate kiss-filled flurry. Easton pulled back a little, giggling, and threw his clothing to the ground behind him. For the first time, Samuel could see Easton's muscular naked back traveling to his strong trunk, leading to one of the juiciest, bubbly asses he'd ever seen. Feeling electric, a sobering thought grounded the moment.

"Are you... it's ok if you're not ready." Samuel asked, feeling certain checking in again was better than not this time around.

"I know. And it's ok if you're not, either." Easton replied, kissing Samuel's neck.

"I'm. I'm ready. I just want you to be comfortable. That's all that matters right now." Samuel moaned.

"I am. I don't have my bottom surgery yet. But we don't have to do anything... there. If that's ok with you?" Easton asked, pulling back a bit to face Samuel with urgent eyes.

"It's absolutely ok."

Both men stripped fully down to their boxer briefs, taking each other in while still passionately enraptured between locked lips, nipped necks, caressed chests. For the first time, Samuel saw the slight, tell-tale faded scarring outlining Easton's impressive pecks. Holding each other tightly in the dark room lit by moonlight streaming through the curtains, both men leaned on the other's forehead. Samuel was grateful the chaos and confusion of the weekend had finally faded and all that lingered was mutual love and longing.

"I think I'm falling for you, Easton." Samuel whispered.

"I hope so," Easton responded, his tone gruff, his eyes locked and fiery.

"I really am."

"Then *can* we wait? Just a little longer? Because I am too. I'm falling for you Sam. And I want this so bad. I do. But can we just hold each other, just cuddle, kiss tonight. Just be with each other as us? Ourselves? For the first real time. Take slow. For now? Tonight." Easton pulled away a bit, biting his lip. Samuel understood. And didn't want Easton to worry he'd be misunderstood again. He wanted to prove he was always listening and paying attention now.

"Yeah. I'd like that. I just want us to be here, together. I just want to be with you, Easton, we can take things as slow as you'd like as long as we do them together. Okay?" Samuel pulled Easton closer and hugged him before continuing to kiss his neck slower. He lingered near Easton's ear to udder "You're in the driver's seat, baby."

"Oh, Sam. I'm not as worried about slow, I just want things to simmer for a while, I like when things simmer. And I also like to drive in life and in bed." Easton started kissing up and down Samuel's neck softly.

"Simmering is *very* good." Samuel moaned, pulling Easton closer.

By morning, Samuel awoke still in an entangled embrace with Easton in the warm white bed. Soft sunlight poured across the bed through the sheer inner drapes of the room. He rolled over to kiss Easton good morning, before getting up to order room service and two coffees to go. They packed up and devoured breakfast still half-naked in the privacy of their room.

Samuel settled the bill at the reception desk before they headed to their rental SUV, giggling and flirting.

"I took a moment this morning and added you to the rental policy." Samuel winked, handing Easton the keys.

"What?" Easton laughed heartily.

"You heard me last night, you're in the driver seat, babe." Samuel's eyes glinted, before planting a wet kiss on Easton's perfect lips. Both men sighed happily as they climbed into their respective seats. Leaning over the console, Easton kissed Samuel softly on the cheek and neck. Samuel grabbed his hand tightly as they pulled out the packed parking lot.

Unlike the ride into the Midwest, the ride back home to DC was joyful, bright, exciting, and informative. Samuel shared his hopes for his career and even mentioned he wanted to eventually introduce Easton to his mom and dad. Easton agreed they'd make one hell of a DC power couple, both on and off the field. Samuel talked about Rachel and warning Easton she could be biting at times, but a true pushover at heart. Easton shared his story of coming out—both times—and that his Auntie will likely fall in love with Samuel after getting to know him better.

Over many miles, salty snacks, and sweet drinks once again, both men were this time inquisitive and enthusiastic about who the other was, while hopeful and excited about who they might become together moving forward into the great, incredible unknown.

ABOUT THE AUTHOR

Ben Bisbee is a dreamer, a doer, a madman with focus, he considers himself the good kind of dangerous. A mixed genre, multi-format author known for both fiction and nonfiction alike, Ben spends most of his time writing about BIPOC, and LGBTQ+ characters just living their normal lives or having extraordinary adventures and unpacking wild mysteries among the mundane. He's a sucker for misdirection, suburban fantasy, and getting in a reader's head. Ben lives in Ohio with his amazing husband of almost twenty years and their twelve (yes, 12) cats.

Can't get enough of the guy? Visit benbisbee.com